T0196454

BEHIND

DEAD EYES

Kim Leonard

authorHOUSE®

AuthorHouse™
1663 Liberty Drive
Bloomington, IN 47403
www.authorhouse.com
Phone: 1 (800) 839-8640

Published by AuthorHouse 11/03/2017

ISBN: 978-1-5462-0136-6 (sc)
ISBN: 978-1-5462-0135-9 (e)

Library of Congress Control Number: 2017911411

Print information available on the last page.

Contents

CHAPTER 1

A new day began for Kendra with the soft, warm breeze of a long-awaited summer. Yellow wildflowers were blossoming, swinging back and forth in the soft breeze, with their petals stretching, yawning, and reaching for the bright sun's rays. The perfume they produced was heavenly to Kendra's nose. Delicious waves of dark-green field grass swayed with the rhythm of the wind. Everything was a paradise to Kendra as she gazed out of her small bedroom window while still lying in bed. The sun's rays were exceptionally bright for a morning sunrise, burning her eyes and forcing her to shut them tight. The heat from the sun flowed through her body, making her want to stay in bed longer.

Kendra was feeling so excited that morning that she paid it little mind. Today was her first day of vacation from her job as an English teacher for high school students in a tough suburban region. Though she loved her students dearly, she was mentally ready for a summer break. Starting with a long yawn and a complete full-body stretch in the softness of her satin sheets, Kendra began her day. After one more stretch, she forced herself to sit up in bed, her toes reaching the sapphire satin rug that lay so nicely on her small bedroom floor.

This was the first apartment that Kendra and her husband, Aric, had rented as a newly married couple. They had begun to outgrow it quickly and were now eagerly looking for a home of their own with hopes of starting a family.

Kendra dreamed about decorating her new home in the primitive style she once saw in a magazine while waiting for her hairstylist to finish. She became so excited when she thought of a house of their own—a home rather than a small apartment, where she could grow old together with her husband. That day, Kendra and Aric were planning a visit to her mom's to stay for a couple of days. Kendra's mom lived in a beautiful home in the rural area of Long Island, the same home that Kendra had grown up in. Kendra had also been looking at houses close to her mom's. She knew her mom had been feeling lonely without her dad, who had passed away several years ago from an aggressive strain of lung cancer. Sadly, her mom had never gotten over it; she still had all his belongings in their home and wouldn't part with even the simplest things, such as his toothbrush or shaving cream. Kendra worried about her mom and prayed she and Aric would get news about a home they had placed a bid on close her mom's house.

The smell of bacon cooking tickled Kendra's nose; Aric was making a Sunday breakfast. She so looked forward to a special breakfast every weekend.

"Hey, hon, are you ready for breakfast? It's almost done. Get your sleepy ass up!" Aric yelled from the kitchen toward the bedroom. "We want to get an early start on the long drive to see your mother; I'm sure she's missing you."

As she stood up, a wave of nausea hit her like she had

never felt before. It was like being punched in the gut. Thinking that it might be just a simple flu bug, Kendra didn't want Aric to cancel the trip to her mom's. "On my way, honey!" she yelled back in a weak voice as she waited for the nausea to pass. Kendra was planning on getting a pregnancy test as soon as she could without Aric knowing— just in case it was the flu. She smiled as she thought to herself that she might be having a baby.

After a quick shower, letting the warm water wash away the nausea, and then breakfast, she was feeling a lot better and was ready to go.

"Aric, do you know why the sun is so bright today? It's burning my eyes when I look toward it," Kendra said as they finished up breakfast.

"It's weird you said that, Kendra. Before I went to bed last night, I noticed how extremely bright the moon was; I also heard a loud boom from the sky. I thought it was lightning and thunder," Aric responded.

"Probably the ozone layer changing," Kendra responded as Aric gave the kitchen one last look after cleaning up.

The kitchen now all clean, they packed clothes and other necessities into their Geo Metro, knowing when they got to her mom's, they would need to use her dad's SUV for vacation. It had more room in it than their car did for all the camping gear. Vacation was a campsite in Canada that Aric had booked at the end of the winter, making sure they'd get a spot.

"Ready, Kendra?" Aric asked as he finished packing up the car.

"On my way," Kendra yelled at the front door. The last thing she grabbed was their sunglasses; she knew they would need them.

"Ready, honey! Let's go!" Aric said as Kendra sat in the car.

The Brooklyn-Queens Expressway was extremely busy even though it was a Saturday morning and wasn't rush hour; there were cars going in so many different directions, trying to outpace each other just to get to the front of the line, going way over the speed limit. Kendra was amazed as she watched the traffic playing its own little game of "Who is faster?" Aric drove a little too fast himself, along with the ongoing traffic, trying to get to Kendra's mom's house a little quicker while also wanting to get off the highway. Kendra said to Aric in a worried voice, "It seems so many people are leaving the city and not so many going toward it. I have no idea why there is such busy traffic for a Saturday. It's never like this when we go to see Mom."

Aric tried to reassure Kendra by putting the radio on so she could listen to music and relax a bit. Aric had been noticing Kendra had not been feeling too well for the last week or so but hesitated to say anything to her, thinking it might be something going around in school before she left. Kendra sat upright in the seat, feeling a bit more comfortable just thinking about her mom and all that she had gone through in the last couple of years. She knew her mom wasn't being herself; she had noticed it when they spoke on the phone. During a conversation, her mom would forget what they were talking about, and Kendra had to remind her of the topic more often lately as they spoke. It would be a relief to see her mom in person. It had been too long.

They finally pulled into the driveway at Kendra's mom's house after a hectic three-hour drive. Kendra was relieved to be off the highway and away from all the traffic. Mattie, Kendra's mom, was waiting for them on the front porch, smiling happily. Kendra ran up to her mom and gave her a huge hug and a kiss on her cheek. She noticed that her mom had lost a bit of weight. She could feel the bones on her back. It broke Kendra's heart to note that her mom had gotten thinner since the last time she had seen her.

***

As they sat on the patio chairs on the front porch, Kendra gazed into the spacious front yard, remembering all the colorful flowers that used to grow around the old maple tree where she had hung a tire rim and would swing all day long. Both the tree and the swing were no longer there; the maple had fallen over in a windstorm many years ago.

Kendra's dad would plant fresh vegetables that would grow on the side of the house, where the sun was at its brightest during the day. Kendra loved to pick carrots and potatoes for her mom and help her cook dinner. Growing up in her parents' home was always so peaceful and quiet; that is what she dreamed of for her own little family.

Kendra looked at her mom and said, "Mom, it's so nice to see you. You look wonderful."

Aric unpacked luggage from the Geo Metro, which they had purchased the year before.

"Mom, let's go inside while Aric unloads the car; it's a little hot outside. Maybe we can get something to drink, since it has been a long drive here." Kendra was once again feeling a wave of nausea but was trying to hide it so her mother wouldn't notice. As she sat on the overstuffed couch with the matching pillow that was her dad's, Kendra felt a little bit better after just lying down for a few minutes.

"Mom, where do you want me to put the luggage—in Kendra's room again?" Aric asked Mattie in a soft voice.

Mattie didn't answer.

"Mom, where do you want me to put our luggage?" Aric repeated in a louder tone, unsure if Mattie had heard him the first time.

"Place them in Kendra's old room, if you please," Mattie replied after several moments of silent hesitation.

A few hours passed by quickly as they talked and reminisced about everything and anything under the sun. Kendra and her mom began to make dinner together, but she noticed her mom was forgetting the main ingredients in the stew that they had made together for years; still, she didn't mention anything. After they had finished up a feast of beef stew and fresh-baked bread, Aric mowed the lawn and took care of a few other chores that were needed around the house. These included fixing a loose window frame and picking up garbage that had accumulated around the house. He placed it in the front of the yard to be picked up by the garbage men.

As the sun was setting, Kendra noticed that it was still extremely bright—unusual for this time of year. Kendra, Aric, and Mattie sat on the front porch, drinking cool lemonade that Mattie had made earlier. Kendra was sitting in a wicker chair with her legs lifted to her chin. Her arms were wrapped around her legs. She was looking deep in thought and started giggling to herself.

"What is so funny, Kendra?" Aric asked as he watched her laugh silently to herself.

"I remember the time I picked up a huge worm from the garden we once had over there," said Kendra, pointing to a broken fence directly in front of the house. "I wanted to keep it as my pet, but my dad made me throw it back into the garden, telling me it was hungry and it wanted to eat the carrots. I was mad at him for days after that and refused to eat carrots for a long time, thinking I was taking food away from the worm," she responded.

Aric and Mattie laughed together.

"Mom, it's getting dark out. We're going to go inside and lie down now. It's getting kind of late," Kendra said as they got up and headed into the house.

Mattie responded, "Okay, honey, I'll see you in the morning. Get some rest." She turned and walked toward her own bedroom.

Walking into her old room, Kendra's tears of sadness began to fall. Sitting on the bay window her dad made for her as a child, she realized how much her mom must be missing her dad. "Aric, I don't want either one of us to die and leave the other alone." Her tears flowed down her face as she looked out of the bay window toward the rising moon.

Aric held her as he sat next to her. They leaned on the bay window together. "We won't leave each other. I promise together forever. Pinky promise," Aric said as he comforted Kendra, holding her closely in his arms. Lifting her face toward his with his hand under her chin, Aric kissed her lips softly, tasting her sweetness.

"Can we visit my dad's grave before we leave, please, Aric?" Kendra asked with tears still streaming down her face.

"Of course, Kendra, we'll visit tomorrow, I promise." Aric made a mental note to himself not to forget to take her. Lying down in her old bed, both Kendra and Aric fell fast asleep, holding on to each other tightly.

CHAPTER 2

Kendra was down on her knees on top of the wet grassy grave, reading her dad's tombstone, just wishing she could hug him just one more time. The inscription written on his stone made her heart break. Kendra heard a low whisper in her ear. "You are more beautiful than all the flowers in the world to me. Always remember that," Kendra's dad whispered to her through the breeze.

Kendra whispered back, "I love you too, Dad," as tears fell down her face.

Mattie, who had been standing next to Kendra, bent down and lifted her by her arms into her own arms and let her cry on her shoulder. She played with Kendra's hair like she did when she was a little girl.

Aric put his arms around both women to comfort them. All three slowly walked toward the exit of the cemetery, holding on to one another. As Kendra looked around, she noticed more people than usual were walking around, visiting the gravesites of loved ones. Some were walking weirdly as if they were drunk, uncoordinated in their steps.

But she paid them no mind. All Kendra wanted to do was go back to her old home.

Aric also noticed something was different about the visitors' walking, but he did not say anything to Kendra about it. He just kept his eye on those around them.

"Aric, what is that stench in the air. It smells like a dead animal or something worse." Kendra asked, feeling sick to her stomach as her mouth began to water from the odor. Fearful of vomiting, she walked faster than her mom and Aric to get to the car and leave.

"Might just be the fresh dirt smell from a caretaker digging a new grave. Seems kind of eventful here today. It is kind of busy," Aric replied, knowing that it reeked way worse than dirt, but he didn't want to panic the girls. "Let's just go home, my pretties." Aric embraced them a little tighter after he caught up with Kendra. Kendra and her mother both smiled at him and walked out of the cemetery together.

After another long day passed, Aric and Kendra were feeling exhausted and were ready to get some sleep—or thought they were—when they heard a bang in the kitchen.

"Aric, wake up! What is that noise?" Kendra was shaking Aric viciously.

"What the hell are you talking about? I didn't hear anything!" Aric snapped at Kendra, as she had startled him from a deep sleep. Aric put on the pants that he had previously laid on the floor before going to sleep. *Bang!* It sounded like pots and pans hitting a stove.

"What the fuck!" Aric yelled out loud this time.

Walking slowly into the kitchen as quietly as he could,

Aric held his breath. He could smell smoke, like something was burning. Aric tiptoed a little faster into the kitchen.

"Who is it?" Kendra asked in a low voice from the bedroom, which was right next to the kitchen.

Aric didn't answer as he walked slowly into the kitchen.

"Aric, you startled me, darling." Mattie stood next to the stove with all the burners on high and a huge pot on an open flame. Noodles were in it without water. Mattie had a strange look on her face.

"Mom, what are you doing awake? It's three in the morning," Aric asked, his body still shaking from thinking it was an intruder in the house.

"Oh, honey, I thought you might be hungry. Harold will be home from work soon, and I know he'll be hungry," she replied in a strangely hoarse voice.

Aric ran to the stove, shut off all the burners, and opened the back door. He threw the charcoal noodles out into the backyard onto the wet grass. After placing the burned pot in the sink and running water into it, Aric turned around to Mattie, who had a look of confusion on her face as she sat at the kitchen table, wondering why Aric had just thrown her dinner out the back door.

"Mom, what were you thinking? It's three in the morning. Why are you trying to cook dinner?" Aric asked with concern.

"Mom? Mom, are you okay? What were you thinking?" Kendra asked her mom gently as she walked into the kitchen, opening windows to let the smoke out.

"I'm sorry, honey. Sometimes I get a little confused, ever since that little ant bit me on my knee. I think it caused me to feel sick. I didn't mean any harm," Mattie replied with tears in her eyes. Mattie knew her memory wasn't good at times but didn't want Kendra and Aric to know. She did not want to go into a nursing home. She believed she would feel better in a few days after the swelling went down in her knee.

Kendra's heart was beating so hard in her chest she thought it would come right out of her from all the excitement. She gently took hold of Mattie's left arm and walked her mom back to her bedroom. "Mom, lie down and get some sleep," Kendra said as she tucked her mom into her king-size bed. "Aric and I are in the next room in case you need us. I love you, Mom." Kendra shut off her mom's bedroom light as she walked slowly out of the bedroom, her heart sinking. She wished her mom was okay. But now seeing her mom the way she had tonight, Kendra knew she had to help her somehow before she hurt herself or someone else did.

"Aric, we need to do something with Mom. She is going to set the house on fire or something. She feels really warm." Kendra was now crying in Aric's arms as they lay on her childhood bed. Aric, reassuring Kendra, gave her a compassionate smile and held her the rest of the night. Aric knew Mattie was no longer herself, and this worried him as much as it did Kendra.

Sleep was short-lived as Aric began coughing from the smoke in the house. Aric ran into the kitchen, and there was Mattie cooking on the stove, now with a different pot with no food in it. Aric shut all the pilots off again and took the knobs off. Kendra ran into the kitchen, screaming at Aric. "We need to take her to the hospital to have her checked out tonight! She's burning up!" Kendra said in a panicked voice.

Aric and Kendra got dressed, and then Kendra dressed her mom. "Mom, we're going to the hospital. I'm worried about you," Kendra said as she was dressing her mom. Mattie showed no sign of any emotion. She didn't even talk to Kendra. The moon was ever so bright, Kendra noticed, as she kept her face toward the window, not wanting her mom to see her crying.

***

After all the lab work and numerous tests, the doctor finally came in to talk to both Kendra and Aric. "I feel it's in your mother's best interest to stay here for a couple of days so we can run more tests on her. I'm not sure what's causing her confusion and disorientation, and at this time, her temperature is high. The nurses just gave her some Tylenol," Dr. Leon explained with expressive concern for Mattie.

Kendra kissed her mother's forehead before she began walking out of the hospital room. "Aric, take me home. I don't feel so good. I want to lie down for a bit." Kendra's face was pale.

"Okay, let's go! We'll learn more about your mother in the morning. Let her get some rest since she will be safe here," Aric said as he wrapped his arms around Kendra's shivering body to try to warm her up a little bit. The night was unusually cold.

Back in the emergency room, it was filling up fast since they first got to the hospital. Patients were coughing badly; some of them were coughing up blood into old rags with pale faces. Aric held Kendra tighter and walked faster through the swinging doors toward their car. They left the hospital as fast as they could. Aric helped Kendra into the car, shut her door, and looked back toward the front doors of the hospital. He saw people inside the emergency room, screaming and fighting with each other. Aric got into his car and drove little faster than the speed limit, taking Kendra back to her mom's house.

Kendra lay in her bed while Aric cleaned the kitchen up and opened more windows. By this time, the sun was rising, and a cool breeze was welcomed in the house to help get some of the smoke odor out.

Aric walked into the bedroom slowly and quietly so as not to wake Kendra up if she was sleeping. Slowly, Kendra turned around toward Aric.

"Are you feeling okay?" Aric asked with concern.

"I am now, honey. I just needed a little rest," Kendra said as she rubbed her belly. "Come lie next to me so we can get some rest. Aric, we have a long drive tomorrow," Kendra said as she smiled, knowing they were going camping the next day. All the camping stuff was packed in the back of her dad's old SUV.

She continued, "I called the hospital early this morning. Mom is doing better today, and I think it would be good for us to go camping. Dr. Leon was making rounds. His nurse will let me know how Mom is doing. They are planning on keeping her a few days. She is in a safe place, and the charge nurse has my cell number if she needs to get a hold of me." Kendra's voice showed her excitement. She was anxious to go camping and fishing and spend time in the woods with Aric. She was waiting for the right moment to tell Aric he was going to be a daddy. This made Kendra's face light up with happiness.

***

All packed and ready to go, Kendra took a last glance at her childhood home with a feeling of sadness about leaving her mom in the hospital, at the same time knowing she would be safe. Less than halfway to the camp, Kendra's stomach began to growl. Knowing she was hungry, Aric looked for a place to eat. He drove quietly, not wanting to speak about what he had seen in the emergency room the night before.

***

Dr. Leon and his nurse Cathy were walking together down the hall toward Mattie's room.

"Doctor, did you hear the commotion in the emergency room last night?" Cathy asked.

Dr. Leon replied, "I wasn't on call last night, so I went home to sleep. I haven't heard anything yet." Walking into Mattie's room, Dr. Leon approached her. "How are you feeling this morning?" he asked gently.

Mattie turned to face him with eyes that were so white they could have glowed in the dark. Snarling at the doctor and his nurse, Mattie rose from the bed, pulling herself with the same arm that had IV fluid infusing. Dr. Leon notice the arm was half chewed off, only hanging where the forearm met the upper arm by a thread of skin. Mattie's mouth was full of blood that drooled out with every snap. She moved toward the doctor and his nurse. Dr. Leon tried to run out of the room, but Mattie, even at her age, was quick, catching up to him in a flash and grabbing his white coat. She dragged him to the floor, where she bit into his pulsating artery and began chewing on his neck while the nurse screamed and screamed in horror as blood splattered on her uniform and face. Mattie walked slowly toward her.

CHAPTER 3

"This looks like a nice homey place to eat, Kendra," Aric said as he looked at the sign, which read "Home Cooking," and smelled the scent of an apple pie baking. It made his stomach begin to rumble. He continued driving toward the old restaurant where the smell was coming from. Standing in the doorway, a waitress showed them where to sit in a booth by the window.

Kendra sat on an old chair. The stuffing was wearing down, and she began moving her bottom back and forth to get comfortable. She could not get over the noxious scent in the restaurant. It was as bad as the cemetery. As a child, her parents took her here once for a special dinner. Back then, it smelled different, like delicious baking apple pies, not death.

The waiter came to the table to offer Kendra and Aric a menu. As the waiter placed the menus on the table in front of Kendra, she asked, "What is that odor?"

"I'm not so sure, miss. I think it smells like some kind of animal is close to the restaurant not feeling too well. Would you like to move to a different table?" the waiter offered, but Kendra declined, taking a sip of her ice water.

Being pregnant, Kendra was not able to stand the horrid odor. Standing up from her seat and pushing the menu away from her, Kendra was ready to leave before ordering anything to eat. "Aric, I can't eat here. The smell is bad."

They walked out of the restaurant to be hit in the face with a horrendous stench of death, worse than when they first arrived.

The drive to the campground was slow. Kendra was eating potato chips from a convenience store that Aric had bought when he had stopped for gas while she was asleep. "I am feeling better now. I needed that nap and something in my stomach. Thanks, hon." Kendra sat up in the car seat, feeling much better now that the odor was no longer in the air.

Aric turned the radio on, scanning different stations, but he was only getting static. "Funny, I can't find a station. I only wanted to know what the weather was going be this weekend." Aric was getting frustrated, changing the stations furiously.

"Just leave it off for now. It won't work because we are in the valley and there are a lot of mountains around us. You're probably not getting good reception," Kendra told Aric firmly, like a parent scolding a young child.

From then on, the drive was smooth. There was no traffic to be seen either way, which Aric thought was odd. Being a holiday weekend, the roads should have been busier. Finally, maneuvering the tuner back and forth for five or so minutes, Aric found a station with country music, Kendra's favorite kind of music. She hummed to the tune.

Kendra's favorite song came on, and she sang as loud as she could along with the song. Aric laughed, enjoying her offbeat singing.

A news caster suddenly came on in the middle of the song. "Hello to all my country-loving fans out there. Looks like it's going to be warm and sunny this weekend out there, so get your gear and get out and enjoy! The summer, folks, is finally here, Yahoo loves—"

The radio was abruptly cut off, and the static came back on. "What the hell is that all about?" Aric said out loud.

"Just leave it off till we cross the border," Kendra said.

Aric and Kendra sat in silence for the next few miles. The static was louder on the radio when Aric turned it back on. A male voice was trying to break through, but it was cracking in and out badly. Neither Kendra nor Aric understood a word the news caster was saying.

Kendra noticed the water under the Peace Bridge toward Canada was flowing slowly with black, foaming ripples of dirt floating on top of the water, which was not normal, especially for this time of year. Aric began to search on the radio for a station to hear music or something other than static. The ride was getting to be long and quiet going to Canada.

The radio made an awful noise. It finally tuned and made a loud *beep*! Beep! A male voice came over the radio. "Please excuse the interruption, folks. A few words of caution for campers this weekend. There have been reports in the areas of the surrounding campsites that raccoons have been attacking, going after any animal. Several dogs have been severely attacked; some of them were attacked so badly they had to be euthanized. So keep all your pets close at hand at all times. Raccoons were always friendly creatures; they usually come out for food when hungry and then leave the campers alone. If you or a family member has been bitten, go to the nearest emergency room immediately! There is no known reason why the attacks are happening. Be cautious out there, folks. We will be releasing information as we receive it. Stay tuned to this station for further updates. Pay special attention to their eyes; they are white, which is not normal for a raccoon in the area. Once again, folks, have a great weekend, and stay clear of any animal that might look rabid.

Aric looked at Kendra as her face became pale. "Don't worry; we'll be fine since we don't have any animals with us." Under his breath, he said to himself, "Thank God, we don't."

Kendra just looked straight ahead with an expression of worry on her young face, not saying a word to Aric as he drove.

"I wonder what is making those things bite. They are usually friendly, or rather just steal food and run." Aric was hoping to himself they were still like that at the campsite or were friendly.

The radio station continued to beep, and Kendra lowered the volume. Aric felt the car tire shake on left passenger side, as if he had run over something. "What the fuck is that?" Aric yelled as Kendra jumped in her seat. "Stay in the car!" Aric warned her as he pulled over to the side of the road. "Whatever it was, I think it's dead now. From that putrid smell, it's probably been dead for a while." Aric looked at the animal he had hit and thought to himself, *What the hell kind of animal is that? What did I run over?*

The small animal resembled what was left of a cat. The thing was moving weirdly, making a screechy moaning noise from its mouth as it lay on a pile of its own matted flesh. Walking slowly toward the animal with caution, Aric noticed its eyes were abnormally white and cloudy. This was not normal for any animal. The rabid animal lay, curled up in a ball as if it were protecting itself from harm, blood was coming from every orifice of its little body.

Aric grabbed a stick and tried to move it by poking at its stomach, to see if was still alive. The rabid animal's head stretched like a snake as it snarled and snapped at Aric's hand, taking a small, fleshy piece of his forefinger as he was still holding the small stick. Aric jumped backward, the animal reached with a severed paw and scratched him on his left hand.

Kendra screamed, "Oh my God!" She ran from the car and grabbed the bandages that were in the suitcase they had packed for the trip. "I told you to stay in the car, Kendra!" Aric spoke as Kendra wrapped his hand with bandages firmly to stop the flow of blood from the small bite. After she cleaned the minor wounds and wrapped them up, Aric and Kendra both returned to the car, walking slowly, looking around in case there were any more of the rabid animals.

Aric's hair stood on end as the animal's eyes watched him as they slowly walked away. Every bone in its body looked broken from Aric running it over. The thing was unable to move on its own but could twitch its body back and forth. The snarling was getting louder as it attempted to move toward Aric, snapping its rotten and broken teeth. Aric keep his eyes on the animal. He wanted to put it out of its misery.

As soon as he thought it, he knew he didn't want to scare Kendra. The animal was hideous, and the smell was horrid. Most of its body was still stuck to the wheel of the car. Aric faced Kendra as he spoke to her. Seeing the fear in her eyes, he could have kicked himself, knowing how much she loved animals.

"We have to put this thing out of its misery, honey." Aric took the branch he used to poke at it and forcefully jabbed it in the head, ending its horrid life.

CHAPTER 4

The rest of the drive was quiet, each one lost in his or her own thoughts. Kendra looked up. "Greenwoods Campsite, 2 miles ahead," the sign on the highway read. Kendra's mood became more relaxed. She was looking forward to camping. After hitting the animal and crossing the busy border, Kendra was ready for some rest and relaxation and needed to check on Aric's hand.

"The radio said we should go to the hospital, Aric," Kendra said as she looked at Aric's hand. She did not notice blood on the bandage. It looked like it had stopped bleeding.

"Let's get settled in first and then talk about it, Kendra," Aric replied.

Aric was glad to be at the campsite, just to get out of the car to walk and stretch his long legs out.

"We are finally here," Kendra said aloud as she got out from the car and stretched her own legs. "It is beautiful here, Aric. Look at all the campers. We're going to have a great time here; I just know it." Kendra could not hide her delight. She was like a young child on Christmas morning.

She continued to look around the campsite, taking in the beauty of the flowers and all the luminous colors that surrounded the campsite. The multicolored roses were in full bloom, giving off the sweet scent of their perfume. It was so strong they smelled them throughout the campsite. At the entrance, to the left, was a beautiful Victorian home that the owners of the park lived in. But it didn't look like anyone lived there now. It was quiet and a little bit unkempt around the gardens at the entrance. The windows were huge, and there were so many of them the house looked like it had faces staring at them. The brochure on the campsite stated the house was haunted by passed-on family members. It was an unusual sight. Kendra was going to make sure Aric walked her around the grand mansion.

"I'm going to get us checked in. It will only take a minute or so," Aric said as he started walking toward the general store.

Kendra knew in her heart this was the perfect place to tell Aric the happy news about the baby. As Aric walked out of the general store, a bell chimed. Kendra needed to go the restroom badly.

"Aric, can you walk me to the restroom please? I don't want to go alone."

They walked hand in hand toward the public washrooms, observing the beauty of the campground. A group of teenagers walked by wearing bathing suits, smiling and giggling on their way to the huge swimming pool. It was a perfect day to go swimming. *Lucky for them*, Kendra thought to herself. She made a mental note to ask Aric if they could go swimming after they settled in. It would feel really good, as the day was getting warmer and warmer.

There was country music playing somewhere in the campground, and Kendra was singing to the tunes. Aric felt like a kid again as he was setting up the two-man tent he had purchased on sale at Christmas. He knew he was going to make good use of it, he thought with a proud smile on his face. Aric always was one for a good deal, sort of a penny pincher, but he'd never skim when it came to Kendra.

Kendra was sitting on a stone bench under a huge maple tree with a smile as big as the Grand Canyon, full of joy. She listened to the kids playing and running in the nearby fields, making all kinds of funny noises, screaming, and laughing. A family of four next to them had just finished setting up their campsite. The woman looked at Kendra.

"Hi, my name is Jane," she said as she introduced herself. Kendra's new neighbors had two sons, she noticed. They were sitting on another bench, playing cards. One boy was about ten years old. The older one was an annoyed teenager who had better things to do than play a boring game of cards with his little brother. The expression of disgust on his face was priceless.

They both left the bench, leaving the cards on the table without putting them back in the box.

"Boys will be boys," said the mother with a smile, picking up the cards and placing them back into the card box. "It is so beautiful here that we have come every year since we gave birth to our oldest son. It has become a family tradition."

Kendra hoped she could find a family tradition of her own and keep it going for years and years to come.

Jane appeared to be a nervous woman. She looked worn out and tired, like she had done all the work with little or no help from her family. Kendra wondered what kind of husband she had.

Aric set up the fire pit as Kendra brought out the hotdogs. They both were hungry, and it was getting late. The day was moving fast. The sun was beginning to set on the horizon. After Kendra and Eric ate hotdogs with potato chips and orange soda, Aric cleaned up, making sure all the food was in the airtight containers they had taken from her mom's home. Kendra sat on a cut log close to the fire pit, feeling as warm inside as she was outside. She just loved being there with Aric.

Aric sat on the log next to her and wrapped his favorite blue wool blanket around her. The fire was beginning to go out.

"Let's go to sleep, Aric. I'm so tired from all the driving we did today. Besides, we have the whole week to enjoy ourselves."

As they were standing up, a bright light shown on them from an oncoming park cart.

"I'm sorry if I scared you younger folks. My name is Charlie." Charlie looked like a much older version of Bruce Willis. "I am the caregiver of this here park. Have been here for the last forty years! I'm just wanting to let you folks know if you need anything at all, just let old Charlie here know. Also, I ask that you don't feed the raccoons. They have been a nuisance in the campgrounds early this year, and the nasty things have multiplied by the dozens. I have been catching and getting rid of those damn things. It must have been a cold winter," Charlie said with a smirk on his face, not wanting to mention he took five dead raccoons out of the pool that very morning. "Make sure all your garbage is wrapped up tight and your food remains in tightly closed containers. There is a huge dumpster down the main road you entered from.

Please make sure the dumpster lid is down after you throw your trash out. You folks have a great night, and remember, if you need anything at all, just asked old Charlie here," Charlie said as he got into the cart once again and drove off.

"Thank you, Charlie!" Aric called out as Charlie drove away.

"He was a bit weird, in a friendly way," Kendra said. She watched the headlights on his cart fade away as he drove off. As Kendra looked up, she thought to herself, *This is the perfect ending of a perfect day.*

Aric held the tent's entryway open for Kendra to get in and then zipped it after he followed her inside. As the camp was settling down, the crickets' solos were making their own beautiful harmony.

After Kendra slowly went into the tent, with the help of Aric holding her hand, he began to undress her. He wanted to make passionate love to her as his manhood was encouraging him for some relief. As he admired her beautiful naked body in the darkness of the tent, Aric became more aroused, putting a smile on Kendra's face. "Kendra, I love you," Aric whispered softly into her ear. He guided her down tenderly onto the inflated twin air mattress.

Kendra wanted so badly to tell Aric about the baby they were having but didn't want to spoil the passion of the moment, so she decided to wait until after the lovemaking. Aric began kissing her ear and her neck, exploring her body with his hands. They made passionate love into the late hours. They fell asleep and remained so until they heard talking from outside of the tent.

***

"Aww, Mom, why can't I sleep in the station wagon like Michael?" the younger of the two brothers whined, trying to get his way, as he usually did. "I'm old enough now! You used to let Michel sleep in the wagon when he was my age. Mom, please, please!" he continued to beg his mother.

She was getting frustrated and didn't want to make a scene in the campsite. She knew the other campers heard her son's whining. She was nervous they would come out of their tents and say something to her.

Jane gave in and let him sleep in the station wagon like his older brother, knowing well enough he wouldn't stop begging until he woke everyone in the park.

Kendra thought to herself, *I bet he gets scared and wakes up in the tent with his parents.* She smiled to herself, attempting to return to sleep. Everything became quiet once again, but the horrid odor seeped into their tent, keeping Kendra awake and making her eyes water and her nose itch. She turned over toward Aric, who was sound asleep and kissed him on his forehead. Covering her face with the blanket, she turned on her left side and once again tried to go back to sleep.

***

Jane was not able to get any sleep either, as she tossed and turned in the tent. Harold, her husband, said firmly, "Go back to sleep, Jane! You worry too much. The boys are fine for heaven's sake!"

Jane was still wide awake and unable to sleep. Feeling like taking a little walk in the warm air, she left the tent and her snoring husband alone.

Michael was sleeping in the tent; his younger brother was alone in the car. Jane walked into Michael's tent and began to shake him. "Michael, wake up! Go sleep with your brother. I don't want him sleeping alone out there in the car!"

"Geez, Mom, he wanted to be alone out there. I slept alone when I was his age. Just leave him be. I don't feel too good anyway. My head hurts a lot," Michael responded in a weak, lazy voice.

Jane touched his forehead and noticed he felt a little warm and then felt horrible for yelling at him. "Okay, get some rest. I will see you in the morning. I love you. Night, honey," Jane commented as she left the tent.

Jane started her walk toward the back of the campsite so she didn't wake anyone else up. Looking in on her younger son before she began her journey, Jane found he was snoring softly. She knew he was okay. She just worried too much, just as her husband had told her. Jane knew she did, but that was what moms were for. Men didn't understand and never would.

***

Michael couldn't go back to sleep after his mom woke him up. He thought, *Maybe if I sleep in the fresh air in the car next to my pain-in-the-ass brother, I might get some sleep.* Michael was used to taking the brunt of all the bad things his brother did, since he was the older one and always knew better, even when he didn't know what was going on. He had learned to accept it growing up. Jane was always rough on him for being the older son and expected a lot from him.

"Fresh air my ass. It stinks like shit out here," Michael said to himself as he exited his one-man tent. "It smells like something rancid died around here." Wrapped in his sleeping bag, Michael walked toward his parents' station wagon. He crawled in next to his brother. Michael yelled at Mark, "Move the fuck over! Mom is making me sleep with your sorry ass!"

Michael pushed his younger brother over, as he was cocooned in his sleeping bag and wasn't moving of his own free will. Mark gave a low, cacophonous roar as he was moved over slightly to let Michael into the back of the car.

"Mark, wake up, man! What the fuck is your problem, little dude?" Michael was staring at Mark's forehead, which was the only body part exposed. His brown, wavy hair was saturated with a sweaty, foul odor. Michael was getting nervous as he shook his little brother. He looked over to his parents' tent and wondered if he should wake them up or not. He didn't know his mother had gone for a walk alone a few minutes earlier.

Jane came back from her walk at the same time Michael was debating on waking her up and letting her know Mark didn't look so good.

"Mom, feel Mark's forehead. He's burning up!" Michael yelled as he saw his mother walking toward the car. Jane walked to the car to check on Mark, feeling his exposed forehead with the back of her hand. She noticed that he was still sweating profusely, and his skin was hot to her touch. "It must have been something that the both of you ate today. Maybe it was the fish fry you had for lunch on the way here. Try and get some sleep; you both will feel better in the morning," Jane told Michael as she climbed back into her tent hopefully to get some rest like her sound-asleep husband.

Jane crawled onto the air mattress, feeling it begin to

slowly deflate as she rested her body next to her sleeping husband. He turned over away from her. She just rolled her eyes in frustration and covered herself in blankets, praying to herself that the next day would be better. She hoped no one would be tired and cranky from the long drive. In her head, she planned on making a huge breakfast and inviting the young couple next to her tent to join them. Feeling exhausted, Jane finally fell fast asleep with her back toward her grumpy husband.

Jane woke up abruptly to the awful noise her husband was making. He sounded like a bear stuck in a cage that was starting to get out. "Harold? Harold, are you okay? What is wrong? You're scaring me. Please stop," Jane pleaded with her husband while his whole body was shaking uncontrollably, like he was having a grand mal seizure. She tried to hold him down.

Harold sat up slowly as his body moved in a jerking motion on the air mattress. He was face to face with Jane. His cloudy, white eyes were looking at her. Now petrified, Jane tried to move backward, away from him, toward the opening in the tent. She smelled the rancid odor coming from Harold's mouth. It smelled like rotten meat. As he moved closer to her, there was a devious grin on his face. Tears streamed down Jane's face as she tried to let out a scream. Harold grabbed her forcefully by the shoulders, pushed her down, and took a massive bite deep into her neck with his now rotting teeth. He aggressively tore open the soft, sensitive skin on her neck. As his teeth reached for her carotid artery, his sour tongue licked her blood. Harold clamped onto her carotid artery, suckling it as an infant suckles its mom's breast for milk.

Any attempt Jane had to scream was now pointless. No sound came from Jane's mouth, other than the gurgling noise she was making. The only sound that came from the tent was the grotesque sound of Harold eating his wife, which no one heard.

CHAPTER 5

The normal routine every night was getting really boring to Charlie. It was the same old thing—welcome newcomers; make sure all fire pits, which were made from old tire rims, were out by midnight; and check that no one was on the playground or the pool after hours. The teenagers always loved to go skinny dipping when all was quiet in the camp and all the campers were asleep. The water was always at a seventy-degree temperature. It was, therefore, so inviting at times, or the hot tub was a famous spot for those who were drinking too much and wanted to take a little nap. They often fell fast asleep. He prayed they didn't drown.

Even though it was early morning hours, Charlie could not sleep and decided to check on the park. Walking into the play area, he saw all was quiet—a little too quiet for a summer's night. He continued walking around, checking his normal spots for anything unusual. All was standard except the redolent, horrific odor coming from the behind the swing set. Charlie walked away, ignoring it, knowing he had traps set up for the raccoons the night before, if the little fuckers dared to show up. But for the time being, they were empty. The only thing left on the trap was a little blood. "Off to the next site further down toward the pool," he said aloud to himself as he got back into his cart.

Slowing his cart down to a halt, Charlie parked it by the swimming pool. "Sure stinks like shit around here tonight," he said aloud to himself. Charlie got off his cart and walked into the small lobby off to the right of the pool, which was used for pool storage, and turned the pool lights on. A low buzzing sound started as the lights began to come on; Charlie knew that sound well. It was the motor to the pool, cleaning it of debris throughout the night. Then it automatically shut itself off in the morning before the swimmers got there. *Hopefully, no more dead raccoons got into the pool*, Charlie thought to himself.

Charlie checked the lobby. It was one of his jobs to make sure it was clean for the next day's upcoming events and to put all the chairs on the tables. Charlie walked through the lobby into the main pool section. As he knew it all along, the pool had teenagers in it splashing, swimming, and having way too much fun. "Okay, young ones, let's get out of the pool now. You know there's no swimming after dusk!" Charlie yelled to them as he walked toward the pool.

They acted like he wasn't even there, other than to reach out and try to grab him. No one attempted to climb out of the pool or respond to what Charlie was saying to them. He walked closer to the pool, noticing the unusual cherry shade to the pool water, which was unusual. "What the hell did you kids do to the pool?" Anger rose in Charlie's voice. "Get the hell out of the pool now before I have to call the fucking cops on your asses!" he shouted to the unhearing teenagers.

Looking down into the pool by his feet, Charlie saw a

severed hand floating, moving in circles. Jumping back a couple of steps and holding his breath, horrified, Charlie watched the hand jerk back and forth in the water. He knew this was a horrible joke. He gazed at the kids. They were not swimming, and some of them were sinking to the bottom of the pool, trying to get back up to the top. Others were just splashing around, trying to get out of the pool, moving toward him.

"What the hell?" Charlie screamed as he continued to back up in shock at the repulsive sight of the three dead teenagers in the pool. He tried to grab his cell phone to call for help while the stench was growing stronger, making him gag. They tried to swim closer to him. The hairs on his neck stood on end, warning him, letting him know, someone or something was behind him. Feeling uneasy, Charlie began to sweat. It poured down his back. The moon had disappeared behind a cloud, and the sky was black as Charlie looked up.

Turning only his head around slowly, Charlie came face to face with a teenage zombie! Charlie knew this teenager. He came every summer with his family. He was a smart kid, never any trouble. "Hey, kid, it's me, old Charlie," he said, hoping the kid would recognize him, but he didn't. Charlie looked closer at the kid. The skin on the right side of his face flapped when the kid made any movement with his head. It was repulsive, making Charlie want to vomit then and there. His eyes were milky white without any pupils. He moaned as his mouth opened wider than any human could have opened his or her mouth. The kid reached for Charlie with his bloody arms, and blood dripped onto the cement floor of the pool in front of Charlie.

The thing's mouth opened unnaturally wide, and the stench-laden air that came out of it looked like the steam of foul gases coming out of a train's engine. The stench was sour enough to make Charlie want to pass out. Its teeth were rotten with shreds of flesh dangling in between them. Slowly backing away from the zombie, careful not to fall into the pool, Charlie took little soft steps so as not to offer any reason to excite the zombie to attack him. The kids in the pool were moaning. It became louder and louder. They knew there was a fresh meal close, but they couldn't get to it.

Another zombie staggered behind the kid. Its movement was slow, awkward, and uncoordinated, as if it were intoxicated. "Okay, Charlie, it's time to get out of here," Charlie said in a horrified voice out loud to himself as he ran back into the lobby, slamming the door shut behind him. The dead teenagers were right on his tail, following right behind him. The dead teenager banged on the door. Charlie thought they were going to break it down before he could escape out of the lobby.

Reaching into his front pocket, Charlie grabbed his phone and dialed 911. He only got a busy signal. Charlie redialed and redialed, but all he got was a continuous busy signal. Giving up, Charlie ran toward the campers to warn them of the walking undead, praying that they would believe him. If not, they could look right behind him and see for themselves. Charlie tripped over one of the raccoon traps he had set out the night before and fell into a pile of green ooze, which was all that was left of the raccoon it had caught that evening.

The dead raccoon or whatever was left of it came crawling toward Charlie; the thing was crazed, screeching like mad, snapping its furious little canine teeth at Charlie. Charlie screamed in horror as he ran toward the owner's house to warn him and then the campers. He was not thinking clearly, for there was no one in the house. Chase and his family lived in a camper not far from the house. The camp staff had not reopened the huge house yet for the summer season.

Vigorously rubbing the slime off his sleeve with the back of his hand, he noticed it was a sticky, bloody ooze that smelled like something grown in hell itself. Charlie ran toward the owner's house. Running up the long steps to the dark house, Charlie felt a bit out of shape; he was trying to catch his breath and forcing his legs to go on. He was banging on the old maple door and ringing the bell repeatedly, but there was no answer. Charlie kicked over one the patio chairs and threw it at the zombie that was now coming after him with its mouth drooling like that of a dog about to get a meaty bone. It was right behind him now, getting ready for the tasty flesh it was about to eat.

"Help me, God! Please, God! Help me!" Charlie screamed. Unfortunately, no one heard him. Charlie ran around the circular porch. He prayed the zombies weren't smart enough to go the other way and meet up with him. Sweat was pouring off Charlie's face and running down over his eyes. It was hard for him to see, but he continued banging on any window that he passed and knocking over the pots of flowers that he was so careful to water every day, all the while screaming like a madman, but still no one heard him.

Charlie, they are not there! You're a stupid, old fool! Charlie thought to himself as he ran off the porch and prayed he didn't run into another one of the damn things. Looking around, he concluded he was lucky to get away from the teenagers for now, Charlie knew they were right behind him and would catch up sooner rather than later.

CHAPTER 6

Chase, the owner of Greenwood's Campsite, wanted to make it a safe and fun place for people of all ages during the warm summer months. Chase's mother had given him the campsite in her will after she passed away five years earlier. Chase had made so many changes to the campsite, like expanding it and building new cabins. It was becoming a well-known vacation spot to visit between Canada and the United States. Chase was so proud of himself for all he had done in the camp and knew his mother would be extremely proud of him too.

From time to time, Chase liked to walk the campgrounds at night. He loved smelling the new spruce trees that were now budding. In the past two years, Chase had become obsessed with planting various kinds of trees, knowing that he was planting too many. He just kept planting more and more of his special trees. It was a compulsion he had always had, even as a child, to own more than he needed.

Walking toward the general store, he saw all was quiet. The lights were out, but Chase could hear noises coming from behind the store. He knew the noise was not from where he had walked from. The campers knew no one could be in the pool after midnight. It was in the manual all the campers were given! Even the ones that came year after year received a manual every time they arrived. *Well, if I run into Charlie, I will have him go with me to talk to the obnoxious kids. They would listen better if two adults confronted them*, Chase thought to himself.

A few of the campers were empty. It wasn't the peak season for most seasonal campers. The housekeepers were getting them ready during the day as Chase knew, because the small windows were open to let in the fresh air. Taking a break from his short walk, Chase sat on one of the small benches that belonged to that part of the camp and wondered where the horrid smell was coming from. He sniffed the odor deeply, trying to determine where it was originating.

Leaning back on the bench with a smile on his face, Chase was happy with life, thankful to his mother for all she had given him as he looked around the park—the house, the land, and, of course, all the money she had saved all her life for him. He dozed off briefly and awoke abruptly, jumping to his feet at a loud squeaking noise. Chase knew the campsite was full of various rodents, though he didn't mind them too much. That was why he, as a lover of all animals, had planted so many trees for them to live in.

Chase heard the screeching again. It didn't sound familiar or like any animal noises he had ever heard on his nightly walks. Chase decided to look around one of the campers, believing the noise was coming from behind it. Looking behind the camper, he saw a trap and expected to see a raccoon caught in it. He had warned Charlie several times to never put traps around.

What he saw was a raccoon fighting to get loose in the trap that Charlie had put out. "I will have a talk with that man when I find him," Chase said aloud to himself in rage. He walked up to the trapped raccoon and saw only the tail had been snagged. "I will help you, little one." He looked down at the raccoon and felt remorse for it. It looked like it was in excruciating pain. Its eyes were bulging from its little head like they were about to burst out. "Damn you, Charlie! I will have your ass for this!" Chase thundered. He had known about the countless critters reproducing in the park during spring, but he only wanted them caught in a cage and humanely disposed of.

Chase detected the unique smell of death as the raccoon moved its body toward him. The raccoon jumped at his face with his tail still attached to the trap. It ripped a chunk of skin from below Chase's left eye and down the side of his face, leaving bloody facial muscles exposed and dripping with warm blood. Chase screamed in agony from the burning pain of half his face being ripped off. The raccoon leaped toward Chase's face again, knocking him off balance. He fell to the ground. Chase grabbed at the bloody animal to pull it off his face. He looked at its mouth and saw his very own eye in it. Grabbing the rancid raccoon and slamming it to the ground, Chase screamed piercingly as he held onto what was left of his face. He stomped on the animal and beheaded it, watching his very own eye pop out of its mouth and roll away from him.

***

Emma heard screaming. She lowered the television's volume to hear it better. Knowing Charlie would be home soon, she was always scared alone at night and stayed awake, waiting for Charlie to finish his nightly rounds. Emma turned all the camper lights on, as she usually did when alone so she could see better outside of the camper windows. She shut the TV off and prayed Charlie would hurry home soon. Smelling a redolent odor that was coming into the open kitchen window in the front of the trailer she was looking through, watching for Charlie to come home, she whispered to herself, "Charlie, please come home. I'm scared."

The front screen door flew open from a strong breeze, bringing a foul smell with the wind. The camper was an older one, not in very good shape anymore. Emma's mom had bought it from a friend for their wedding present. The trailer had cracks here and there, and it was cold in the winter, but it still held up strong. Emma jumped up as the door banged back and forth. She hit her head on the stovetop that she kept bugging Charlie to get rid of because it was so old and rusty and about to just fall off one day while she was cooking dinner. It no longer had a purpose in her kitchen. The kitchen was too small to begin with, crowded from years of storing things they didn't need any more or use. But Charlie was a hoarder, like his mother, though not as bad. Emma was always throwing Charlie's things away without his knowledge. She screamed when she heard banging on the front door after it closed shut.

Charlie was standing by the door, banging and screaming. "Emma! Emma, open the door!"

Emma ran to open the door.

Charlie knew she was up because all the lights were off so she could see outside better at night. Opening the door,

Emma yelled, "What is all the screaming about out there, Charlie? You scared the life out of me!"

"Get inside and shut the door now!" Charlie said breathless. "Look, Emma, I don't know what is happening out there, but people are dying and coming back to life. I just saw a few kids in the swimming pool dead and still—oh my God—trying to swim as if they remembered how to. Lock the door! Shut the blinds! Keep the lights off!" Charlie screamed at Emma.

Emma's mind was trying to comprehend what Charlie was saying. He was unstoppable with his words, and Charlie didn't believe what he was saying himself. He grabbed Emma by the shoulders and shoved her into the small bathroom and into the tub. He held her tight out of fear and a desire to protect her. Listening to the screams and avulsion going on outside right next to their very own door, Emma and Charlie cried in each other's arms, sitting in the small bathtub with only the warmth of their bodies holding them together for comfort.

"Charlie, are we going to be okay? I am so scared!" Emma was crying softly as she spoke to Charlie in a low voice. Emma put her head to rest on Charlie's chest. He leaned back against the small bathtub, trying to regulate his rapid breathing as the screaming was getting closer and closer to their camper.

CHAPTER 7

Michael was rubbing his little brother's back, trying to comfort him since their mom had left them to go back to sleep with their dad. Mark's face slowly poked out of the sleeping blanket like a worm exiting from the dirt, looking around, wondering where it was. Mark's eyes were white and milky. He snarled with only one side of his mouth, drooling. He looked at his brother with copious amounts of saliva hanging from his mouth.

"Mark, what is wrong you?" Michael's lips were shivering in fear as he spoke. Mark didn't say a word. He began to convulse violently, still wrapped up in the sleeping bag, Michael held onto him tightly, praying to himself that Mark would stop convulsing, praying to himself that his mom would come and check on them again that night.

Michael slid his body toward the back of the station wagon to get a better look at Mark. Mark's breath was raspy. His breathing was quicker, and the convulsing had stopped for the time being, but Mark was unresponsive. The only parts of him moving were his tongue and eyes. Michael ran to his parents' tent for help for Mark. As he got closer, he saw his mother crawling on her knees as she came out of the tent toward Michael.

"Mom, something is wrong with Mark!" Michael said slowly as he approached her. Something was not right with his mother. Jane stood up with her arms reaching for Michael as if to hug him, but her gait was tottering, as if she were drunk. His mother never drank anything stronger than coffee.

Jane was shuffling her feet toward Michael as the left side of her face was twitching violently back and forth. She was stepping closer and closer to Michael like a madman.

"Mom? Mom, is that you?" Michael asked with tears streaming down his face. "Please, Mom, you're scaring me! Stop it!" Jane was only a few steps away from Michael. It was then he noticed the blood on the front her nightgown, dripping down like a small river on an embankment after a thunderstorm.

Jane began to snarl at her son like a rabid animal about to attack its victim. Half of her neck was missing, and the blood poured out of her neck like a worn-out garden hose leaking water. Jane ambled closer and closer with her arms stretched out as Michael backed up further away from his mom. He grabbed a broken branch that he had nearly fallen over. He began to swing it back and forth in front of himself as his mom moaned.

Michael looked behind himself to see if Mark was okay, but he was no longer in the station wagon. Mark had climbed out of the station wagon by himself. Backing up, Michael tripped on something soft. When he hit the ground, Mark was crawling toward him with a face looking like a wounded animal's, facing Michael with his now demonic eyes. Practically nose to nose with Michael, Mark was snapping his teeth and growling like a rabid animal.

Just as Michael opened his mouth to scream, Mark lunged at him, jumped on him, and ripped out Michael's bottom lip with his fierce teeth. With fearful eyes, Michael watched as his brother chewed and swallowed his own lips. Feeling the blood pouring out of his mouth, Michael got up to run and ran smack into his mother, who grabbed him by the shoulders and knocked him down.

Jumping on Michael, Jane tried to gnaw his chest as Mark grabbed his left leg and tried to bite into it like he was about to eat some rich corn on the cob. Michael lay there in shock, unable to move. The only sound came from his mouth, the gurgling scream of shock in the back of his throat as his mother and own brother chewed on his flesh. Michael's last vision of his life was his dad coming to join the smorgasbord with the rest of the family.

***

Aric was sleeping soundly, snoring as he usually did when he was tired. Kendra didn't mind. She was glad he was getting some rest, finally. She noticed that he had bled through the fresh bandage she had recently applied. The first-aid kit was right where she had left it. It was at the edge of the blanket before they went to sleep. Kendra grabbed and opened it to apply a new bandage.

As she reached for it, Aric turned over on his left side. Kendra noticed she could see the hand better with the light from the moon shining. She removed the dirty bandage while Aric slept and placed it on top of a small pile of dirty clothes. She noticed some green-colored, thick, vile serosanguinous drainage coming out from the scratch on his hand. Kendra was noticing a few raised blistered areas that were not there before the raccoon attacked him. Knowing that was not normal for any wound, Kendra tried to wake Aric up. Finally, after five minutes of shaking and calling his name, she managed to wake him up.

Aric, waking slowly, asked, "Hey, what's up, Kendra?"

"Aric, look at your hand! It's badly infected. We need to get to the hospital now," Kendra said in a concerned voice with tears in her eyes from worry. She continued to unwrap the rest of the bandages from his hand.

Aric looked down at his now badly infected hand. "Nah, it's not that bad, Kendra. Just put a new bandage on, and we can go see a doctor in the morning," he replied. He knew the emergency room would cost a fortune, being out of state with no health insurance especially there in Canada, and remembering how packed the emergency room was back home, he knew it would be just as bad here.

With lots of pleading and begging, Kendra got Aric to finally agree to go to the hospital. As she was packing up all the important things they might need, Aric began to moan about his hand hurting like hell. It was turning beet red, and numbness was setting in. The blisters were filling with bloody secretions. Aric touched one, and it exploded, spraying thick, serosanguinous fluid. Kendra rewrapped it for the third time. The drainage was filling up the bandages faster than Kendra could change them.

Kendra unzipped the tent screen so Aric could get out. He was now bent over in agonizing pain from the wound. Half holding Aric up with what little strength she had and dragging him, she headed to their car. Opening the passenger door, Kendra told Aric, "Aric, get into the car. I'll drive," Kendra begged him as she helped him into the front passenger seat. Aric still did not want to go to the hospital.

Kendra heard footsteps from behind her as she lifted and put Aric's feet into the car. Hearing the muddy footsteps, Kendra turned around. Jane, one of the campers from the next tent, was staggering toward her. She had half of her neck dangling down and no mouth and was bleeding profusely from everywhere, as if her face had gone through a meat grinder.

Jane was making weird gurgling noises from what was left of her mouth. Kendra didn't understand her, but from looking at her, she knew she needed help. Michael was behind his mother, staggering toward Kendra as she backed away from him. She was still holding on to her husband, who no longer had the any strength left. She shut the door for her husband and ran around to get into the driver's side of their car. Michael was right behind her, reaching out for her.

Kendra, petrified, yelled at Michael, "Get away from me. Please get away from me!" Michael followed Kendra to the driver's side as he reached for her with long arms stretched out. Opening the driver's door, Kendra jumped into the driver's seat of their car, eagerly trying to start the engine. Her heart was pounding so hard, as if it were trying to jump right out of her chest. When the car started, she backed up the car fiercely. Feeling bad about leaving the kid behind, Kendra knew there was something wrong with him. However, her husband was more important to her, and she needed to get him to a hospital.

Aric started shivering next to her. Kendra grabbed an

extra blanket that they had in the backseat and covered Aric with it as she drove. She was pushing down on the gas pedal to encourage the car to go faster. She began to sweat profusely out of fear for her husband. He needed to get to the hospital and fast. Aric was bending over in his seat, and Kendra was unable to see his face anymore, but she knew he needed medical attention.

"Hang on, honey! We're almost there," Kendra said, panicking, as she knew well enough they could not get there any faster. Bang! The back of the car hit a huge maple tree extremely hard. Kendra had not seen it in the dark. Her neck snapped back and forth rapidly, like a Ping-Pong ball going back and forth on the table.

Aric didn't seem to have felt anything thing other than that he was on the floor in the front seat. Kendra shook herself to get of all the spider webs out of her brain. Her neck hurt badly! The pain was intense! Ignoring it, she went into fight mode for her husband.

Kendra started the car again, but the engine didn't turn over. She tried again and again. As she looked out of her window at the huge house that belonged to the owners of the park, she begged God to let someone look out the window to see her and help her. Kendra stepped slowly out of the car, making sure the doors were shut so Aric won't try to get out. She walked to the huge Victorian house faster than she had ever walked before in her life. She pounded with all her strength on the door, but no one answered.

Kendra then walked back to her car. Leaving the doors shut so no animal could get to Aric, she kept the driver's door unlocked. Kendra was almost near the car when she noticed how steamy the inside of the car had gotten. Getting closer, cautiously, Kendra considered the driver's seat window. The moon was full that night, shining into the window. Kendra's heart beat faster than a horse racing on a racetrack.

Stepping closer, a little at a time, scared out of her mind, Kendra moved forward. Looking at the window on the driver's side again, Kendra saw green ooze mixed with blood smeared on the window. Aric was moaning loudly in the seat. As Kendra got close to the window, Aric jumped up and put his face to the window, licked it, and growled at her with blood oozing from his mouth. In a state of disbelief, Kendra screamed, "Aric, *no!*" Aric's face was in a state of pure rage! He snapped his teeth and growled at Kendra, trying to break through the window, banging on it with his bloody hand.

Not believing what she was seeing, Kendra jumped back and fell over a rotten tree branch. She landed on her back. With her hair swinging around her face, she quickly looked around her in fear. Kendra began praying to herself that someone would be around to help her. Her hair was wet with sweat and sticking to her face. Back on her feet, she ran. Kendra didn't know what direction she was running, but she kept running as if hell were chasing her.

Aric continued to scream and moan inside their SUV, deranged and agitated that his meal was getting away. All the windows in the station wagon were up; there was no way Aric could escape the locked vehicle. The car rocked back and forth with his rapid rage. Kendra ran so fast she didn't see Chase pass her heading toward Charlie's camper in a mad rage.

***

The wind began to pick up at the campsite. The windows in Charlie's camper were shaking from the strong breeze. Charlie walked toward the tin door slowly. He heard his wife say, "Charlie, what should we do?"

"I don't know. I'm thinking of what to do though," Charlie replied. "Stay in the bathroom, and don't leave until I tell you to. I'm going to look around and see what is going on out there and if there's a way for us to get the hell out of here."

"You are not leaving me here alone! I'm going with you!" Emma insisted.

"Fine, suit yourself, woman," Charlie replied with a bit of anger in his voice.

"What is that loathsome smell?" asked Emma, now annoyed with her husband.

"Shut your mouth, woman! Be quiet! You hear me?" Charlie whispered in a low voice to his nagging wife.

The lights were still off in the camper. The only brightness came from the shining moon. He covered his nose and mouth with the old T-shirt he always wore when he used to go to all the races, or as many as he could, with Emma.

The stench was repulsive. Charlie gagged and tasted a small amount of stomach bile in his mouth. He was close to the front door. Hearing Chase's knocking and banging on it, Charlie's hair stood on end. His breathing became rapid. Emma was now hanging on to his T-shirt for dear life, not saying a word, also covering her mouth and nose with a bath towel from the bathroom to mask some of the stench smell in the camper.

Emma and Charlie jumped when they heard a loud

banging on the door. Chase was crazed, banging and yelling, "Charlie, old man, let me in! I need to have a talk with you!" His voice sounded harsh, as if he had swallowed a hot pepper and was unable to speak clearly.

"What do you want, Chase? I am not opening this here door for no one," he replied.

"Open the door, Charlie boy," Chase said in a demonic voice as he banged and slid his nails down the door. Emma and Charlie, standing next to the kitchen sink, tried to peek out of the window to get a look at Chase. Sweat was running profusely down Charlie's back.

Unable to see Chase from the window, Charlie walked closer to the door, grabbing a butcher knife that was on the small kitchen counter. He looked out of the window by the sink. Emma gave him a questioning look. "Just in case, Emma, you stay right close behind me!" Charlie directed her. Emma was shaking in fear, as she held on to Charlie tightly.

Chase pushed the door open with his bloody hands, dragging his body into Charlie's camper, falling face first on the inside steps. Chase's face was gushing blood, which sprayed onto Charlie and Emma. Chase looked up at Charlie with his glossy white eyes, drooling copious amounts of salvia and blood mixed, looking like a melting Slurpee on a hot day. As Chase was dragging himself inside, Charlie grabbed onto his shaking wife and attempted to go around Chase before he got a chance to get up. Emma placed her leg as far away from Chase as she could. Chase lifted his head and, with a bloody arm, grabbed her leg and ripped flesh off it. Emma screamed as she tried to get her leg loose. Charlie, close behind her, grabbed her by her arm and threw her onto the ground outside the trailer so Chase didn't get her again.

"You fucking son of a bitch!" Charlie yelled at Chase as he kicked him in the face repeatedly until Chase was no longer moving, smashing his face completely until his brain matter was scattered all over the steps and inside the camper.

Charlie helped Emma to walk toward the picnic table they had shared since they were married twenty-five years before. Sitting Emma down slowly and carefully onto the bench seat, he began assessing her leg. Emma was going into shock. Her leg, where Chase had ripped her skin off, was bleeding profusely, the blood pouring down onto her foot. Charlie took his shirt off and wrapped it tightly around her wound to try to stop the bleeding.

"Am I going to die, Charlie?" Emma asked as her body shook uncontrollably as if she were having a grand mal seizure.

Charlie held her close to try to keep her calm, knowing what those things were. He knew his wife wouldn't live after being infected by Chase.

CHAPTER 8

"Hold me, Charlie, please. I am so cold!" Emma said with a weakened voice.

Charlie held her tighter, tighter than he had ever held her before. Emma's breathing was becoming labored. Her heart was pounding, fighting for blood supply as she clung onto her husband. When her breathing stopped and her heart pumped no more blood, Charlie gently closed her aging eyes as tears fell down his aging face.

As Charlie laid her on the picnic bench, Emma's eyes flew wide open. She was looking at Charlie with crazed eyes that were totally white. Her skin turned an ashen color. No longer was Emma alive as a being in this world; she was now alive in the world of the dead.

Emma sat straight up, staring at Charlie as he stepped back away from her. A fowl and a decaying odor came steaming out of her mouth. Charlie stepped back with tears flowing freely down his face, knowing he should end her misery but not having the strength to do it. Charlie gave Emma a hard push back as she tried to sit up, so it gave him time to run from her. Emma fell hard onto the ground.

She pressed her hand to her mouth and silently screamed. Kendra looked at Charlie puzzled.

"Girl, the world has gone badly. Everyone is fucking eating each other out there. We are safe in here for now, but I don't know for how long."

In disbelief, Kendra on shaky legs walked over and peeped out of the window. Moving the heavy curtains, she watched the world outside. One large man was chasing a woman and knocked her down. As she screamed and tried to fight him off, the man jumped on her like a wrestler in a fight and began to devour her face and neck, scavenging her flesh. Blood bubbled up, foaming from her mouth as the woman tried to scream but nothing came out.

Another man was yelling in anger in the direction of the walking dead, "Move the fuck over, you animals!" as he pushed the crippled dead out of his way. A smaller framed woman was right behind him, chasing him. She was mad like the others, with blood dripping from her neck and all over her face. As the man reached the door to the mansion, he banged on it and shouted, "Open the fucking door! I know you are in there!"

Charlie and Steve looked at each other, not sure if they should let him in or not.

"I will break this fucking door down!" he screamed louder in a panicked voice.

"If he keeps shouting like that, we are all going to get killed!" Charlie said to Steven and Kendra.

"If we let him in, they will be on us like white on rice, biting us," Steven replied.

"We can't leave him out there," Kendra said in a shaken voice.

The man screamed and ran to the back of the house, beating and kicking and trying to break the back door in. His crazed wife was right behind him. The man had no time to kick the door for the third time, as she caught up to him and grabbed him by the back on his head, biting into the back of his skull, tearing flesh off along with his hair.

Hearing the bones break, she savagely chewed his scalp through the flesh and ripped it from his cranium. The woman was putting her head back and swallowing a huge piece of his flesh, slurping the blood down like a melting ice-cream cone on a hot summer day. Kendra did not believe her own eyes as she watched in horror. She stepped back away from the curtain, her whole body shaking in fear. *This is a nightmare! I'm going to wake up from this soon*, Kendra thought as tears flowed down her face. She closed the curtain and sat on the red chair Steven had been hiding behind. Kendra grabbed a pillow from the chair and hugged it as she watched Charlie and Steven board up the front door.

Charlie and Steven reinforced the front door as quietly as they could with nails that Steven found in one of the kitchen drawers he had looked through earlier as he searched for a weapon. Kendra walked around the house, making sure all the windows were covered. Everything was quiet for the time being. The dead seemed preoccupied and gave up pounding on the door.

Kendra heard a loud bang from upstairs as if something had fallen on the floor. All three of them looked up. Each with his or her own distinct fears, they faced the stairwell.

"Steven, stay here with Kendra. I am going upstairs to look and see what the fuck that noise was," Charlie said.

Steven was happy to stay put rather than go, and the

relief showed on his face. He just nodded his head toward Charlie.

Slowly, Charlie climbed the carpeted set of stairs. Cautiously, he held on to the maple handrail that his boss always wanted to be kept shiny and dusted all the time. Another thump made Charlie jump and skip a step, and he tripped, throwing himself backward a few steps.

"Be careful!" Kendra whispered as Charlie climbed the stairs.

Charlie made it to the top of the stairs. He swore to himself that the pictures on the wall had eyes that stared at him, and he felt the heebie-jeebies. The hairs on his arm on his stood on end.

The second floor of the house had a strong musty odor that tickled Charlie's nose, making him sneeze even though he tried to hold it back not wanting to make any noise. The hallway had four doors, two on either side. Charlie knew these had been the bedrooms of people who used to live there but were now long gone.

Charlie, with his hammer in his left hand, opened the first door to his left with his right hand, turning the gold-plated doorknob with extreme slowness. The door opened with only a slight squeak from the rusted hinges. The room was full of dust angels, flowing in from the window. A huge canopy bed was in the middle of the room. It looked as if no one had slept in it for years. Charlie walked out of the room and gently closed the door. The next door was locked. Charlie looked through the peephole and saw a duplicate of the previous room. He tiptoed to the next door. With his ear on the door, he heard a whisper, sounding like a man's voice.

Charlie knocked on the door. "Who is in there? Open this door, or I will shoot the fucking door down!" Right then, he heard a baby cry at the same time the door flew open. A tall man came out in a hurry. The men stared at each other in surprise.

"Who are you?" Charlie asked the man with a desperate voice. "Come with me downstairs, and let's talk." He spoke to the man, knowing the man was not about to fight him but was frightened of him. A woman walked up behind him, carrying a baby wrapped in a blue blanket.

"Hello, miss," Charlie said to her, and she nodded her head in acknowledgment.

The woman followed Charlie downstairs, along with her husband.

Kendra looked at the woman and noticed how fatigued she looked. It also looked like she had been crying recently. Kendra led the woman to the couch and introduced herself. "My name is Kendra. What is your name?"

The redheaded woman replied in a teary voice, "My name is Lisa. We just got here last night."

Kendra looked down toward the infant and saw that he was happily nursing. She smiled at him.

"I'm sorry I can't offer you anything; we just got here ourselves. How long have you been hiding upstairs?" Kendra asked in a questioning voice.

The woman began to cry uncontrollably. Kendra held on to her and let her cry. As she also cried, the two women comforted each other.

Charlie grabbed the man's left arm. "How fucking long have you been up there? Did you or did you not hear the commotion down here, and why didn't you come down and help, for God's sake?"

The man put his head down and replied, "We have been up there since we heard the report on the local broadcasting station this afternoon. We have two small boys to care for and didn't want to chance one of them being attacked by one of those mad animals. My name is John, and this here is my wife, Lisa, and our newborn. He is one month old today," John said with sadness all over his face.

Charlie looked around the man and didn't notice another child. As he did so, the man replied with tears streaming down his face, "My son was only a child. He was only five years old. I was going to teach him how to fish while we were here. As we ran into the house, a diseased raccoon jumped on his stomach, knocked him down, and bit him. It bit and bit into my boy's stomach. I killed the son of a bitch animal, but it was too late for my boy. My little boy had become deranged like the raccoon and got right up and tried to bite his mother.

"We ran into this house since the door was unlocked. Then we ran upstairs into one of the bedrooms and stood very quiet. I don't know where my boy is now. One minute, he was holding my hand; the next minute … Oh my God!" The man cried, looking Charlie in the face.

Charlie felt so much compassion for him, knowing that it was this man's son that he had kicked in the head and killed. Then Charlie had thrown him out into the lawn like a garbage bag, along with his own wife not long ago.

Charlie looked at Kendra; he knew she was thinking the same thing as the man spoke. He noticed she hugged the woman a bit tighter. Everyone looked at Charlie, waiting for him to decide what to do. Charlie had no idea how he was going to keep everyone alive or what was happening outside.

Charlie took control over their tragic situation. He began to give orders out. "Steven, go upstairs and look out one of the windows on the north and south sides of the house. Let me know how bad it looks out there and how many of those things are out there."

Turning around, facing John, he did not want to ask anything of him, as he was grieving for his little boy, but Charlie had no choice. "John, follow me around the house to help me double-check the doors and windows."

John walked behind him with his head down low. Charlie's heart broke for the guy. They found the front door looked good for the time being with the extra nails he had banged into it. John and Charlie dragged a large metal cabinet from the pantry and placed it firmly against the back door. The china dishes rattled as they moved it, but none broke, surprisingly.

Steven came down from upstairs, his face as white as a ghost. "I don't even know how to explain what is happening out there," he said with extreme terror.

Charlie had never seen anyone in shock so badly as the kid.

"They are eating each other like savages. There is so much blood out there, it looks like one huge red rainstorm," Steven responded in a grim voice.

Lisa and Kendra screamed as the lights in the house went out.

"Calm down and be quiet!" Charlie said in a strong, firm voice. "We are okay for now. The morning will be here soon, and then we can leave, I pray."

The infant began to cry. As Lisa placed him on her shoulder to comfort him, the wailing became louder. The infant was feeling the fears of all in the room and could not be subdued. Lisa walked around the floor, rocking the baby, and then handed the infant to John so he could try to comfort him. Rivulets of sweat poured down Charlie's face, causing his eyes to burn from the salty fluid. Kendra sat on the antique couch with her hands clasped together between her knees, rocking back and forth. Her breathing was rapid, like that of a runner who had just finished a mile-long race and was trying to fill his lungs back up with the air they desperately needed.

Kendra looked quickly behind her, believing that she saw an apparition of her husband. Feeling new strength, she stood and looked at Charlie. "We have to leave here, or we will all die, Charlie!"

Lisa went to her husband. He held her and comforted the infant, and Steven leaned against the door as if his being could keep the undead out. Kendra looked around the room and listened to an area where most of the moaning was coming from.

"Look, Charlie, most of them are in the front of the house. Do you think we can run out the back way? They are going to eventually get in here; I know it," Kendra said.

"This is the end of the world," Charlie said to all at the same time.

The small group huddled together for dear life, each one ruminating in his or her own thoughts.

Everyone jumped as one of the shutters was ripped off one of the windows and the glass broke. The dead were now getting in. Kendra ran to the kitchen to get a weapon. She grabbed a butcher knife off the kitchen counter and ran back to the others. Charlie still held on to his hammer.

John held his hysterical wife and crying infant, and Steven ran back upstairs and slammed one of the doors shut.

"Charlie, did you hear that? It's gunshots! Someone is here to help us! Charlie, can't you hear it?"

Charlie ran for the back door, along with Kendra. He gave one good kick to the door, and it flew open. Both Kendra and Charlie ran out toward the gunshots. John and Lisa ran back upstairs into the room they had been hiding in. The campground was pitch-black except for the bright-yellow lights of the gunfire. Kendra looked back at the house. Fear rose in her stomach as she saw the dead running into the house. She heard Lisa screaming and John yelling. She knew they were both dead now.

Those things were eating them. The infant was no longer crying. Using the moonlight, she followed the sounds of the gunfire. As she ran, she turned for a split second to see if Charlie was still behind her. He was nowhere to be seen. Kendra held on tight to her butcher knife, readying herself for the worst of the worst.

Tripping over a raised tree root, Kendra fell on her face, knocking the wind out of herself for a minute. Her faced burned from the pain as tears flowed down. Kendra tried to rationalize the atrocity going on in the world. Getting back on her feet, she got her bearings back. Looking around at her surroundings, Kendra had no idea which way to go. Every direction looked the same.

No longer hearing the gunshots, Kendra kept going in the same direction, following the light from the moon. To her right, a few feet away, a horde of the dead was surrounding a body that was convulsing on the ground. They were too busy devouring it to notice her. As she looked at the body, she recognized it as Charlie's. "I am sorry, old man," Kendra said sadly. "Okay, Kendra, calm yourself down and think this out before you do anything stupid," she whispered to herself, and she tiptoed away from the hungry horde of undead.

All sounds ceased around her, and the silence was eerie. Kendra felt like she was on another planet, not her own, soundlessly walking through the campground, looking for someone to help her. Kendra knew that life as it was once was no longer existed. She knew that she had to protect the child in her stomach no matter what it took.

CHAPTER 10

All Kendra heard was her own heart pounding loudly. She was running with sweat pouring down her face and wet leaves sticking to her bloody feet. Kendra saw lights from the highway. As she ran toward them, a small group of the dead had their heads up, sniffing the air when they noticed her. Kendra ran away from them as fast as she could, as if hell itself was chasing her. A man no older than she was, running behind her, turned and took a different direction as a horde of the dead ran after him. Kendra ran behind a large maple tree and prayed the sticky branches would hide her.

"Help me! Help me!" the man hollered repeatedly, as the undead were right behind him.

As Kendra hid, she backed up farther into the branches of the old maple tree. Its sharp branches clawed at her face. It felt like fire scorching her face as they lashed at her. Kendra's arms and face were laced and with her crimson blood. As she wiped the blood away, she noticed welts on both her arms from the tree branches, and tears from fear rolled down her burning face, stinging her like salt on an open wound.

Sucking in her breath, she turned around to see if the man was still close to her. What she did see was a pack of gluttonous creatures feasting on his flesh! They were ripping him apart like an old stuffed animal. The man looked at Kendra with pleading eyes. He was still alive. One of the dead tore his arm off and sat apart from the horde, eating it. Kendra knew there was no help left for him now and began to run again. She spit out a mouthful of sour bile from the horrible sight.

Kendra held tightly on to the butcher knife while still praying it would help her if any of those things grabbed at her. Kendra said aloud in a low voice, "This is all a nightmare. That is all this is! I will wake up soon in Aric's arms!"

Kendra knew from visiting the area there were horses not too far away. She ran toward the stall, following the horse scent, thinking if she could ride a horse, it could carry her fast enough to help her get out of the campsite of hell.

Walking slowly into the barn, Kendra noticed the stalls there were kept clean and it was unnaturally silent, other than one horse making a strange noise further back in one of the stalls. As she took her first step into the stable, Kendra noticed horse whips of various colors hanging on nails on a wall off to her left side. She never believed in whipping a horse or any other animal for any reason. As she stepped in further, Kendra saw the arena where the horses practiced. Kendra touched a well-used leather saddle that was sitting on the ground, waiting for someone to use it. The leather was cold to her touch and sent a chill up her arm. There were only ten stalls, but there were millions of flies.

Gross! Kendra thought as she swatted all the flies away from her face. Kendra wasn't sure which stall the horse was in. It continued to make a weird grunting noise. Not knowing much about horses other than what she learned from riding them as a child, Kendra knew that was not a normal sound that the horse was making. It sounded more like agony or maybe labor. She was hoping neither was the case.

As quietly as she could, Kendra walked closer to the stall where the horse was. Kendra's eyes flew wide open, not believing what she was seeing. The horse was lying on the hay, moaning in agony and pain with its eyes bulging out as its owner was chewing on its leg. The horse was unable to stand up, though it tried with all its strength. Seeing Kendra, the horse got excited, thinking she was going to bite on him also. He began kicking the owner and sent him backward, flying toward where Kendra was standing. He flew right through the short wooden door on the stall that prevented the horses from getting out, like a rag doll.

The color drained form Kendra's face. She felt like she would pass out as she turned away from the grotesque sight. Slowly creeping behind her was Charlie, his eyes cloudy white. His torso was gone, and Kendra could see his rib bones. Charlie reached for her but couldn't moan because he had no mouth, just a huge, deep red hole. He reaching for her with one arm. His left arm was torn off, and a portion of his intestines was hanging out from his stomach in a revolting way, swinging back and forth as he moved. Charlie came closer and closer to Kendra. As she turned her body around, the owner of the barn was walking toward her. The horse continued to make unbearable noises as it kicked and banged in its stall, trying to position itself to stand.

Kendra stepped back slowly. The hay was still poking painfully into her feet, which were sore from running from the undead. Kendra had almost reached the stable door when the dead man who had been eating his horse noticed her trying to get away.

Kendra ran out of the barn as fast as she could, not looking back. She ran and ran into the deep woods, not knowing where she was going. She didn't care as long as she got away from the undead.

Kendra's bare feet were caked in sticky blood and hay, but she didn't care about her feet now. She ran in between trees and around trees as the branches tore at her face repeatedly. Not feeling any physical pain, Kendra's only thought was saving her life and that of the unborn child who now grew inside her. Charlie and his newfound friend were still chasing Kendra through the woods. They had more friends with hungry, evil eyes after her too. Charlie was close enough now that he could grab her hair. Kendra noticed his finger was nothing more than mangled flesh and bone as he tried to grab her.

Some of the dead were limp, while others were running after her. As Kendra ran, she noticed cabins ahead of her. If she could get into one or get someone to help her, she would be all right for the time being. Maybe she could relax just long enough for another plan.

Kendra began banging on every cabin door, but she saw no one answer. On a few of them, she tried to turn the knobs, but they were locked. The corpses behind her were slowing down, sniffing the air in other directions, looking for prey. Kendra could get a few feet ahead of them. The undead ran to a cabin that Kendra had knocked on, where no one had answered. The dead were now pounding on the door, knowing there was someone inside. A woman was inside screaming, which agitated the dead even more. They were becoming more aggressive while banging on the door to the camper.

Kendra watched once again in horror as the dead dragged a family outside the cabin not far from where she was standing. After breaking in the door, they began to devour them. A mother, father, and baby were being mauled. Kendra's first instinct was to help the younger boy, who was about thirteen years old, as they dragged him by his legs, screaming.

Kendra took the unfortunate opportunity to run, as she hoped the boy would get away. As she looked back, a zombie was already chewing on his leg and ripping his flesh off. The boy screamed with a sonorous voice, and more of the dead came for the banquet of flesh.

At the next cabin, Kendra walked up to the door, knocked on it, and attempted to turn the knob. Considering walking into the cabin, Kendra looked in the window while noticing a little girl sitting in the corner with her body shaking. Her back was facing Kendra.

"Hello, little girl! Are you okay? I'm not going to hurt you, sweetheart. I am here to help you," Kendra told her.

The little girl's shoulders were shaking from side to side as if she were crying. Kendra stepped slowly closer to her. "It's okay now. My name is Kendra. I won't hurt you; I promise," Kendra pleaded with the little girl. As Kendra got closer to the little girl, she was only a foot away from her, the girl turned her body around in an animalistic way. She was on her hands and feet, like a leopard about attack its prey, and she darted for Kendra.

The little girl wore pigtails. She looked to be five years old. Her body was putrescent with decay. Kendra ran out of the foul-smelling cabin and slammed the door in the girl's face as she was reaching for her. The girl grabbed the doorknob and tried to turn it to get to Kendra. The little girl's face was so close to the door's window that she was steaming it up with her foul breath.

Kendra turned and ran down the stairs as fast as she could. She tripped over another raised root, banging her head on a huge stone. Before the lights went out, all Kendra remembered was praying that she wouldn't wake up again to this nightmare as she saw the little girl lunging at her, showing her snarly teeth getting ready to bite Kendra. The last sound Kendra heard were gunshots not too far away from where she was. She heard voices, but they sounded one hundred miles away.

"What if she is bit?"

"No, she did not get bit! Help me get her up," replied a louder voice.

"Come on, boss! She has blood all over her," the other answered.

But that was the last of the voices that Kendra heard. She was praying to herself that they would just kill her and end all this madness.

Kendra's eyes were hurting from the bright lights shining above her face as someone was shining a flashlight at her. She thought she was now in heaven, hearing voices and unrecognizable noises. She felt disoriented, not knowing where she was. Kendra's heart palpitated rapidly with fear.

Her body was numb and frozen, and she was unable to move any extremity. Her eyelids began to flutter open. She heard a voice from what seemed miles away.

"Wake up, girl!"

Kendra didn't recognize the voice. She tried to ignore it and stay in her restful place of peace and oblivion for the time being. Something had a hold of her arm, grabbing it and shaking it, trying to bite her and yelling at her the same time.

"Come on! Wake up!" the man was yelling at her.

Kendra began to swing at the unknown assailant, kicking her feet in the voice's direction, but she could only guess where they were, hearing voices all around her.

She was feeling so much pain all over her body, feeling like the undead were mauling her body, tearing her apart. Opening her eyes slowly, which were very cloudy, she couldn't see who or what was attacking her. Kendra let out a bloodcurdling scream from the deepest depth of her throat. The floor shook beneath her, making her feel dizzy. It felt like the floor was moving in waves of water underneath her.

Kendra sat up in an upright position, pushing herself into a corner with her hands and feet. Looking madly around her, not focusing on reality and feeling like an animal about to be slaughtered, Kendra couldn't make sense of the voices she was hearing.

"Shut her the fuck up, or she will let those damn things out there know where we are!" a tall man wearing a police uniform said aloud as he was looking through the antique, musty-smelling curtain out of the window. He was looking out for any undead coming toward the building they were hiding in, being a lookout.

Reality was coming back to Kendra slowly, but so was a massive headache. "Lady, you are all right! Stop screaming! No one is going to hurt you." A woman about Kendra's age spoke to her in a low, firm tone.

With watery eyes, Kendra looked at an older male a few feet away from her, noticing he also had an army uniform on.

"Where are we?" Kendra asked in a docile voice with quivering lips.

"We were close by shooting those repulsive things when we saw you running from the cabin. Jake here," he said, pointing to the man at the window, "had to put the little girl down. You fell hard on a tree root, hit your head, and went unconscious. Jake grabbed you, and here we are in the office building of the elementary school on the main road, hiding from those things. It's like a tsunami of those things out there. Where you bitten anywhere? It's the bites that kills, and then it brings you back to a life of hell! My name is Bill. This pretty young lady next to me is Casey. She is a college student, or rather *was* a college student, studying for her degree in nursing, as she was in the army, along with the rest of us here." Casey's face turned red as she blushed at Bill's description of her.

"Casey was in her second year of army reserves when all this began. She joined our squad to help us fight the undead."

"My name is Kendra. My husband and I were camping for the weekend when we heard a report on the local station about the rabid raccoons attacking people. We were careful to stay away from them, but one had scratched my husband's hand and he became one of those things out here."

Kendra put her head down and looked at her stomach. She began to cry uncontrollably as emotion poured out. Casey sat next to her and comforted Kendra by putting her arms around her. This made Kendra feel a little relief, knowing someone cared.

Another woman named Kourtney gave Kendra a quick look over for any bites or scratches. There were no bites but lots of scratches. Kourtney ushered Kendra to another room, asking, "Would you like to wash up and change out of that bloody nightgown? We have extra clothes here."

"There are more of us, actually twenty in all, down in the basement. The school has a shelter in case of an emergency of any kind. Thank God," Kourtney explained. "You can meet them later if you want." She was a nineteen-year-old teenager, smarter than a normal, working as a nurse when all this began. She was planning on becoming a medical student.

"Kendra, in the room to the right, there are clothes and food. Let's get you something to eat."

Kendra didn't realize how dirty and hungry she was until after she bathed in a lukewarm shower and ate a whole bowl of instant oatmeal, which was so good to her taste buds. Wearing clean clothes, Kendra felt like a new woman. A tall blond woman walked into the pantry room they were in, causing Kendra to take a step back in shock.

"I'm sorry I startled you! My name is Sally. I am the one and only nurse around other than my assistant, Casey," Sally said as she smiled at Casey. Knowing she needed her help more than Casey would ever know, Kendra noted that Sally had a bit of humor in her tone of voice, which put a smile on Kendra's face for the first time since the night before.

"I am going to leave you with Sally while I join the others upstairs. If you need me, I will be two floors up, okay?" Casey said to Kendra as she left the pantry room.

"Thank you for the food and clothes," Kendra replied.

Sally looked at Kendra. "I guess you're ready to meet

everyone here, but first I have to check on Alice. She is nine months pregnant and due any day. Her husband was killed by those revolting things out there. So sad what is happening in the world now. God only knows where it started and when it is going to end," Sally said to Kendra in a tearful voice.

As Kendra walked down the school's hallway, she noticed all the windows were boarded up. The hallway had a musty odor in the air, and the walls had been painted a dull white quite a few years before. "Are you up for a little tour? I grew up nearby here, and I attended this school for years. It was always a happy place to come to and learn. But first, let's check on Alice."

Sally talked a lot, Kendra thought, with a smile on her face.

As they walked down the hall, another woman was walking toward them. She was petite in size, but she looked like she could hold her own. As she walked past Kendra, she smiled.

"Julie looks after the pantry. She used to work in the kitchen here and lets the guys know upstairs if we need anything. They try to get it for her. But lately, it had been too dangerous to go out there anymore. The men have not been out much lately. She also makes all the meals," Sally explained to Kendra as they walked down another flight of stairs. Even on the staircase, the windows were boarded up. It was dark, so Kendra held on to the metal railing for dear life as she stepped down the metal stairs.

"How long has this been going on with people and animals dying and coming back to life?" Kendra asked Sally in a worried tone.

Sally responded, "It has been about two weeks. The government kept it low key, hoping the contagion would resolve itself and be limited to only the animals and they could easily terminate them. A lot of the crazed animals were caught and killed, but they continued to multiply like crazy. As the raccoons began to attack humans, the situation got out of control," Sally explained to Kendra with a saddened facial expression. It was then that Kendra understood the severity of the situation.

Kendra walked with Sally into a classroom that was made out like a little emergency room. It had beds in it that were taken from the hospital nearby and some medical equipment hanging on the walls. The front desk was full of packages of medicine and IV fluid and lots of bandages. In a corner, Kendra saw Alice lying in bed, resting, awake. Kendra knew the pain all too well. She promised herself when she got to know Alice a little better, she would tell her what had happened to her and her husband.

"Please, Alice, drink a little water. You don't want to be dehydrated while you are giving birth, do you? It is not healthy for you or the baby." Sally encouraged Alice, as she took a small sip from a mug with an old crack in it, which read "Happy Teacher's Day." Kendra noticed an old sandwich sitting on the bedside table next to where Alice lay. Feeling bad for the woman, hoping she would eat something, Sally kissed Alice on the forehead and covered her back up with warm blankets. She checked the infant's heartbeat. "I will be back soon to check on you," Sally said as she turned and began to walk out of the room.

Kendra made a mental note to herself to stop in and see Alice sometime soon. She stepped down another flight of steps in the darkness.

"You will get used to no lights, Kendra. I promise you," Sally remarked as she watched Kendra holding the side rails as if her life depended on her not letting go.

They walked into the basement, which was set up with military cots, one right next to the other, rather close. The people down there were depressed, looking sad. Kendra thought most of them must have lost loved ones. "We have been down here for a week after Jake and his crew retrieved the cots and some personal belongings for the few we have here."

A few of the people looked up at Kendra with an expression that suggested they were happy to see a fresh face. They silently prayed she had news for them. An older couple walked over, shuffling from old age.

"Do you have any news for us? How is it outside? When can we go back home?" the older man asked Kendra in a frantic voice.

As the people began to surround her for answers, Sally told everyone, "Hold on here, everyone. This is Kendra. She was found the same way as many of us. She doesn't know any more than we do yet." As Sally spoke, the people who were standing returned to their cots. Some were even crying and holding on to each other. The children—Kendra only saw three around the same age—sat on the floor and played with what few toys they had.

"Right across from this gym is a small room, which was used for teacher-parent conferences, but now we use it for meetings. We are going to have one tonight to discuss leaving here or trying to find a safer place."

Kendra asked with a questioning expression, "I thought this was the safest place to be."

"It is, but with twenty people to feed, the food is going

pretty fast. We are only doing two meals a day now. Most of the people who are here are not happy about it."

Walking into the conference room, Kendra noticed a large, heavy metal door where the outside door used to be.

Turning around toward Sally, Kendra asked, "Why is that door so boarded up, Sally?"

"That is the door that many of the undead happened to try to break through, even though it is a metal door, we needed to be sure they couldn't get in. Jake and Bill placed double metal doors on it to reinforce it," Sally replied.

Returning to the gym with Kendra, Sally began to introduce the people to her and gave Kendra a cot for herself with a blanket and a musty-smelling pillow. Kendra was grateful. After a dinner of ramen noodles with stale bread, Kendra lay down on her cot with a warm bottle of spring water. The blanket was rough, not anything like her own at home. This made Kendra cry, knowing where she was and all that was happening around her. She put her head on the pillow and covered herself, though not getting any warmth from the thin, threadbare blanket she was using. Getting ready for a full night's sleep, Kendra turned over. As she did, she noticed three teenage girls all sitting on one cot, laughing and talking to themselves.

She overheard one of the girls whisper to the redheaded one next to her, "I'm bored." Then they all giggled.

Still awake, Kendra noticed Alice wobbling down the steel staircase. Her facial expression was one of someone who had lost the biggest battle in her life. Kendra felt bad for her but was too exhausted to comfort the woman. There were no windows in the gym, making it eerie looking and scary when it got completely dark outside. A few candles were lit to illuminate the room. Alice lay down at the other end of the gym, covering herself up and turning the opposite way, not to be able to look at anyone or have anyone look at her.

"Kendra? Kendra?" She heard her name being called from a distance. "Kendra, wake up. It's me, Jake. I need to speak with you for a second."

"Hi, Jake. I'm sorry. I'm so tired I must have fallen asleep."

"Well, it is kind of late. I myself can't sleep." Jake spoke as he sat on the edge of her cot. "Do you want to take a little walk with me, Kendra?"

"Sure, okay, where are we going?" Kendra asked in a subtle voice.

"We are going upstairs. There are more rooms up there. We can talk without waking anyone up," Jake replied.

***

As Kendra and Jake walked into a small room, Kendra noticed it was a classroom and sat on one the of the student chairs with ease. Jake sat on another chair next to her.

"Kendra, I want to know how you are doing. You were pretty beat up when I saw you last. I know you were not bitten, or you would have changed already." Jake pushed his chair closer to Kendra's, and she welcomed it, feeling good that someone cared for her.

Jake noticed something special about Kendra and knew when he had the chance, he was going to talk to her alone and find out more about her.

"Thank you for saving me, Jake. Why is all this happening? Why is it happening?" Kendra asked, putting her hand on her head as if she had a headache.

"Kendra, I do not know. None of us do. We are lucky to be here and be safe for the time being. I heard from one of my fellow comrades a facility not too far from here was experimenting on animals, mostly rodents, looking for a cure for the swine flu. One of the infected rats escaped and infected a raccoon by biting it and causing the virus to spread from there to other animals and then to humans."

Kendra, hearing all this, asked Jake, "Why? Why would someone infect an animal with the swine flu? It is inhumane, poor little critters." Kendra felt a bit of anger toward the lab personal.

Jake surprised himself by placing an arm around Kendra's shoulder for comfort. And even more surprising was Kendra accepting Jake's comfort.

CHAPTER 11

Jake began telling Kendra the way it was supposed to have been. "Our orders were to quarantine all animals that were found loose, especially domestic outside animals, such as cats and dogs! The owners were upset when we removed the animals from their homes, and some even tried hard to fight us off. The government was forceful about keeping animals inside. If an animal was found outside, we isolated them in the shelter, which was becoming full with all kinds of small animals, and unfortunately, we began euthanizing them. A week after that, the virus could no longer be contained," Jake explained to Kendra.

Kendra said with a sad face, "Jake, that is awful! I feel so sorry for those poor animals. Were they infected?"

Jake continued to explain what he knew, as Kendra listened. "A week ago, one of my best buddies came across a dead deer lying in the middle of the road that looked like it had been run over by a car. As he attempted to move it to the side of the road so it wouldn't keep getting run over, the damn thing jumped up and bit him in the neck. It happened as quickly as a fly moves when someone is about to kill it.

As we watched him get up and shuffle toward us, we knew he was infected with the virus. I could not kill him. I just couldn't do it, but my leader shot him in the head with his semiautomatic." Tears were now falling as rain falls off a rooftop on Jake's face.

Jake took a moment to compose himself. Then he continued, telling Kendra the story as he knew it. "The government had already contained the infected raccoon, but it was too late. The virus was spreading by this time, spreading rapidly. The government called a state of emergency. No one was allowed outside in a five-mile radius of where the facility was. People were living in trepidation. I don't understand why the campsite that you were at permitted people in. Especially if they knew what the dangers were," Jake told Kendra.

As Kendra was taking in all this information that Jake was giving her, tears flowed down her face. She began thinking about Aric, and she spoke. "My husband was scratched by one of those infected raccoons. I watched him become sick with a fever; his hand was infected. We were going to the emergency room, but he started to change and tried to attack me. So I locked him in our car with all the windows up. He banged the windows and screamed like a barbarous animal. He licked the window, trying to get to me."

"Kendra, we will be okay here for the time being. Let's go downstairs to the gym so you can get some rest, okay." Jake wasn't sure why he so apprehensive about Kendra. She gave him the impression that she was a strong woman by the way she spoke to him.

Jake accompanied Kendra to her cot. "Get some rest. I will see you in the morning," he said in a soft voice to

Kendra as he walked across the room and sat down on a couple of wooden crates put together to make a chair.

The fog was thinning out as the night rolled on. The moon shone brightly behind the trees, making them look like apparitions flying in the air, like large bats flying around the roof of a haunted house. These gave Jake tremors up and down his arms as he watched out the windows for any sign of the undead coming toward the school. Envisioning what the world had become scared him even more. Jake was usually restless at night, but for the last few nights, he had been unable to sleep at all.

***

Kendra was lying on her cot now with her eyes wide open. She was in shock from all that had happened to her. Turning on her left side, she finally fell asleep, watching Jake sitting on a stool holding tightly on to his gun. He seemed ready for one of those repulsive things to attack him. Kendra fell asleep, cuddling the ragged pillow for safety.

With the arrival of a new day in hell, the morning sun rising on the horizon shone brightly, fooling anyone who looked at it into thinking it was going to be a beautiful summer day. The air had a horrendous, putrid scent of death and decay. Jake had a folded handkerchief over his nose and mouth as he walked toward Kendra's cot, startling her. He handed her one of his handkerchiefs, nodding up and down with his head for her to put it on her face also. Kendra complied.

"The odor is usually not that bad in here. They may be getting closer," Jake said to Kendra. She was sitting up on the edge of her cot, rubbing her back. "We are going to the group meeting now. Would you like to join us?"

Kendra nodded her head, feeling sick; the odor from outside didn't help any. It took all she had not to puke in Jake's handkerchief. As Kendra and Jake walked up the stairs into the conference room on the second floor, there were five people already there whom Kendra had not seen before, sitting around a well-used plastic lunch table. As they looked questioningly at Kendra, Jake said, "She is with me," to the small group, and they all nodded their heads.

The metal folding chairs were ice cold, Kendra noticed, as she sat down and removed the handkerchief from her face. The odor wasn't as redolent on the second floor as it was in the gym. Kendra sensed the anxiety in the room. Trying not to let it bother her, she repositioned herself on the hard metal chair. Kendra knew their situation was abysmal.

Jake was the first one to speak as he stood up. "This is Kendra, the woman we rescued yesterday in the campsite. Kendra, this is Bill. He keeps count on our weaponry. Sally is our nurse. I think you two met yesterday."

Kendra smiled at Sally, happy to know someone there. "This here is Bill's daughter, Casey. She keeps track of all the people here. She will speak with you later and get a little information about you."

Kendra remembered her to be one of the teenagers giggling on the cot next to the night before.

"Drake here keeps an eye on our water means. He's also our lookout, and Julie here keeps an eye on the food sources. She also cooks our meals. She is a damn good cook."

As Jake returned to his seat after circling the room, he continued to speak to the small assembly, looking at Bill, who had been in the police force for more than twenty years. "Bill, how our artillery supplies holding up?"

"Not very good, Jake! We have enough guns and bullets to save us maybe in only one more attack if the horde isn't too great. We need to go scout and get more before long. Our ammunition is running low, sir."

"Thank you, Bill," responded Jake as he rotated his chair toward Sally and faced her. "Sally, how is our medical supply holding up?"

"Sir, not well at all! I am on my last box of intravenous fluids, and the bandages I'm using are cut-up clean sheets. I have a few bottles of antibiotics but will need more shortly. The sutures kits are holding up, but Alice is due to have her baby any day. I pray it is a normal birth without any complications, sir."

"Keep a very close eye on the baby. That infant is our future." Jake spoke to Sally, and Kendra put her hand on her belly without anyone noticing.

Jake once again turned the opposite way, facing Julie. He knew he wasn't going to receive good news from Julie either but hoped he would. "Julie, how are the food supplies holding up?"

Julie stood up and faced Jake. He noticed the aging in her face from only the past two weeks there. "There is only enough food to last another week if we ration it. As it is now, the people are getting upset that I rationed the food out to only twice daily. Soon, it will only be once daily. I also need help in the kitchen cooking meals for all the people, sir."

Drake stood up next as Jake looked at him. "Sir, the fresh water supply is running low unless we can filter more somehow. I informed the people that bathing will only be once every three days with the minimum amount used." Drake sat back down, feeling like a failure. Jake noticed how grim everyone in the room looked.

"I want to talk to everyone here about leaving the school. The last group of scavengers we sent out last night reported to me. There are others out there cleaning out all the stores of food and the hospital of medical supplies. However, we can send them out further to look, or we can pack up what we have and look for another place to survive."

"I am not going to sugarcoat it for us, our situation is dire. As of now, we can't move until Alice has her baby," Sally said to the group.

Bill stood up to speak. "Sir, our situation is bad; I know this. What if our healthiest people go out and look for shelter and food? We can leave the children here with their parents along with the older couples and Alice, with what food supplies we have until we can find a safer place and return to get them. Of course, Sally will also have to stay here to deliver the baby."

Kendra's heart palpitated, hearing all that was happening around her and not believing it all. All she and Aric wanted to do was go camping for a weekend, not all this atrocity. Kendra held her tears in and swallowed, refusing to let herself cry there, showing any emotions while the group was being strong and trying to survive.

Sally stood up abruptly. "Sir, I can stay and help with the newborn. She will need a midwife. This is her first baby." Sally, still standing, looked at Jake for a response.

Jake stood silent for a few minutes before speaking.

"Sally, are you sure you want to stay behind? We will leave ammunition for you and Drake here to defend yourselves. Are there any questions or concerns anyone has?"

No one answered so the meeting was over.

"We will resume this meeting one week from today to decide. I want everyone here to really think about our survival. We will meet sooner if need be. If anyone needs me, I will be here, checking the windows and doors, making sure all is locked up good and tight."

Jake pulled out Kendra's chair for her. Sally noticed and gave a little grin, knowing he had taken a liking to Kendra. He returned a grin of his own to Sally as he helped Kendra stand up.

Jake and Kendra walked down the long hallway of the school, alone in their own thoughts.

"Jake, can I talk to you about something?"

"Sure, you can. Why is it you look saddened, Kendra?"

"Last night after you left me, I tried to get some sleep. The teenage girls, including Casey, Bill's daughter, on the cot next to me were giggling extremely loudly."

"Kendra, I will have a talk with them."

"Jake, that's not what I'm talking about. One of the girls, the one with the red hair, was talking about leaving this place with the other two girls. She was complaining of boredom. I fear they will leave and get killed out there alone."

"Kendra, don't worry; I will talk to Bill about his daughter, and he will talk to Casey, making sure no one leaves this place for now. Thank you for letting me know. Now let's go get some food," Jake said with a smile to

Kendra as she smiled back at him, feeling a brief moment of happiness.

***

Bumping into Bill, who was checking the doors and windows for loose boards while making rounds, Jake asked if he had a minute to chat.

"I sure do, sir," Bill replied.

Jake explained what Kendra had told him. Bill had a look of annoyance on his face at the idea of Casey even thinking about going outside unprotected. He knew she was stubborn like her mother.

"Bill, take it easy, buddy. Be easy on the girls. Let them know the severity of the outside world as it is now," Jake said as Bill walked away from him, responding to his last words.

"I love my daughter more than anything in this barbarous world. I will not let her or the others go exploring on their own! I promise you."

***

As Kendra lay on her cot that night, she knew Bill had spoken to Casey, as she was giving Kendra dirty looks. The girls were whispering quietly among themselves. The girls did this until the following week, making sure Kendra didn't hear anything. They were also being very unfriendly and rude to her. Kendra avoided them the best she could, knowing they were teenagers.

Alice was now sleeping most of the time. Sally checked on her from time to time. She was concerned the baby had not moved in the last three days. Sally listened to Alice's stomach to try to hear a fetal heartbeat, but there was none. Knowing the next meeting would be in an hour, Sally decided she would tell the others about Alice's condition. Sally believed Alice was going to have a stillbirth and feared for her.

***

Kendra, Sally, Jake, Bill, and Drake sat around the metal table, getting ready to discuss matters relating to the group of people who survived. Bill stood up and spoke first.

"Jake, I spoke to Casey. She is no longer speaking with me now. I know she will come around. I explained the severity of the undead situation out there, and she heard as much of it as she wanted to, sir." Bill let out a gust of air, feeling the anguish of a rebellious teenage child.

"Thank you, Bill. We all will keep an eye on the teenage girls and the other children. They are our future, whether they know it or not," Jake stated as Bill sat heavily on the old metal chair that sounded like it was going to break at any given moment. "I think the best thing to do for all of us is to leave in a small group and search for shelter and food."

All nodded in agreement with Jake.

"It is settled; we leave tomorrow at seven in the morning. We will only take a few of the nonperishable food items we can easily carry. All in favor, raise your hands."

All did, even Kendra. Jake was hesitant to let Kendra travel with them, not knowing if she could kill if she had to.

"I am not sure which direction we will be going, but I know south is where the least of the undead are. I look at that direction every day on my watch time," Jake said to the group.

Kendra looked at Jake pleadingly. "Can I go too, Jake? Please! I don't want to stay here alone without you."

Jake was looking through broken boards out of the window with a pair of NASCAR binoculars.

"Kendra, the world's full of revulsion out there. Life is not as we once knew it. I won't stop you, but I would prefer you stay here and be safe and help Sally. If you choose to go, I want you to always be by my side at all times."

"Jake, I promise. I need to see what it is like out there for myself," Kendra said, even though her heart was pounding and she was feeling dreadful.

Nightfall came quickly for Kendra, as she settled into her cot with the extra rough cotton blanket Sally had given her. Cuddling up was a challenge, nothing at all like home. She wished she could take a warm bubble bath and wake up from this unbearable nightmare. Kendra tried to get some rest, but none ever came as she tossed and turned all night. Finally, she fell into a deep sleep, dreaming she was home in her toasty warm bed with her own blankets, holding on to her baby. He was by her side. She was waiting for him to wake up so she could nurse him again.

Kendra placed the squirming infant to her left breast to nurse him, knowing he was hungry. Her bedroom was in another dimension filled with kaleidoscopic colors, stirring around the room in a ghastly display. As Kendra looked down at her newborn, the blanket fell softly from his face, revealing his facial features. The infant had the cadaverous face of the undead with eyes that glowed in the dark. It also had distorted features. As it stared at Kendra's face, its mouth opened inhumanly wide, with sharp rows of teeth and a protruding split tongue, poking in and out, dripping foamy saliva. It was reaching for the tender nipple engorged on her breast, ready to feed. Like an animal, it was hissing at her, with a redolent odor coming from its mouth. Its tongue reached forward to her tender breast, which now dripped blood from the nipple. Kendra screamed as it bit and held on to her tender breast.

Kendra's eyes shot open. Her mind went one hundred different directions, seeing all the events that had happened in the last week in her head. She was fully awake and was profusely sweating and breathing rapidly. The horridness of her dream rolled over and over in her head, tormenting her as she tried to forget it. Kendra woke everyone in the gym up, and as she looked around apologetically, she still received evil looks from the others in the gym.

***

Sally, hearing Kendra moaning in her sleep, woke up. She watched Kendra as she slept, knowing she was having a nightmare, but she didn't want to wake up her up and scare her even more. So Sally waited until Kendra was fully awake to see if she was okay.

Sally walked over to Kendra and sat on the edge of her cot. With a soft tone, she asked, "Kendra, are you okay, honey?"

Kendra was staring up at the ceiling, straining her eyes as she focused on the cracks in the old chipped drywall, which was in desperate need of repairs and a new paint job.

"Kendra, it's okay. You only had a nightmare; you are safe here with us."

"I'm sorry, Sally, for waking everyone up. It was a repulsive dream I never want to have again," Kendra said as she looked at Sally with tears flowing down her face, not wanting to tell her what the nightmare was about, because she did not want anyone to know that she was pregnant. She knew they wouldn't let her travel with them to look for food and shelter.

"We are all having nightmares. No one can sleep in peace anymore since this life of hell began. The life we have now is a terrifying one. We either die trying to live or never get away from it. Try and get a little more rest; you are going to need it. We will be heading out soon, Kendra," Sally said she pulled her own cot close to Kendra's for reassurance.

Kendra lay back down, though she couldn't go back to sleep, thinking about her baby. Kendra so wanted to tell Sally she was pregnant but didn't. She closed her eyes and tried to sleep. The night was seasonably cold for the end of spring, so Kendra pulled her starchy blanket to her chin and prayed for sleep without nightmares.

***

Jake walked into the gym. His eyes were swollen from a restless night's sleep, and feeling stoic, he wanted to go out and try to find what they inevitably needed. He wanted to find a new, safe place for the people he had felt responsible for the last two weeks. He had not volunteered to take charge of the group himself. The group saw he wore an army uniform and expected him to be in charge. Jake did not want the position of leadership, and he certainly didn't ask for it. But it was up to him and his small group to go and scavenge what they could from the atrocity of a world outside of the school's walls.

Kendra and Sally were wide awake, waiting for Jake and Bill to come for them.

"Good morning, girls," Jake said as he was near the cots where the girls were sitting.

Kendra noticed how tired Jake looked and felt bad for him, thinking to herself she would help him in any way she could to make it a little easier for him to scavenge.

Bill took a step closer. "Let's go upstairs and discuss a matter prior to leaving."

Kendra, Jake, Bill, and Sally walked toward the conference room. Julie was already there, waiting for them. She had a frown on her face, as if she didn't want to go and was upset by it. But she knew in this lifetime, there were no more choices to be made. It was do or die, and Julie wasn't ready to die just yet.

Jake stood up and faced the small group. "I made some decisions last night. Kendra is going with us to help scavenge what we need, and Bill here is also going. He is the best shooter we have. Julie, you are also going; you are a fast runner. We are going to need all the hands that we can get. I spoke with Casey last night and expressed the importance of helping Sally with the people and telling the other older girls they are going to do the cooking. Sally with help them with that also, so that being said, are there any questions."

Bill stood up.

"How long will we be gone, sir?" Jake responded.

"I don't rightly know for sure, but the quicker we get going, the quicker we will be back. Since there are only four of us going, we should be able to travel easier and return quicker."

Kendra, Julie, and Bill walked closely together through the gym toward the metal door. All eyes were on them with thoughts of fear and pity, praying they would return with food and help. Some of the people put their heads down. Kendra didn't know if they were praying or if they could not look at them, feeling guilty for not going themselves.

Reaching the metal door, Bill began to unlock it with the key he held closely on his body for safety. It was the only exit key. No one had the enter key, as Drake was always on the watch, looking for them and checking the door. Bill didn't worry about being able to get back into the school as long as Drake had the key; otherwise, the only way it would open was from the inside of the school.

Jake cleared his throat as he looked at them one at a time. "Everyone hold hands."

As each person held the hand of the next, Jake bowed his head. "Dear Lord, cover us with your love, protect us as we enter the world of abomination. Guide us to a place of safety, and protect those we leave behind. In the name of Jesus, amen."

Everyone in unison repeated, "Amen," as they bowed their heads together.

"Don't let them get the opportunity to bite you. If you get bitten, you are on your own. I will put you down in peace. They are hungry, and they are fast. They do not feel pain." Jake spoke these last words as Bill quietly opened the metal door.

The room had an eerie silence to it. Kendra could hear every breath that she took, noticing they were coming faster and faster with each step closer to the outside world she took.

Bill began to unlock the heavy metal door with the only key they owned. The lock on the door was ancient, so he took several minutes to dislodge the heavy bolt. The door noisily screeched open, worn out from the years of being unused. Bill hugged Casey as she was standing next to him, crying. "Please be good, and don't leave the school. I love you."

Casey cried, "I promise you. I won't, Dad."

Kendra and the others shaded their eyes from the sun's burning rays with folded hands. As she was not used to seeing the sun daily, it burned Kendra's eyes, hurting a bit until she got somewhat used to the brightness. She was wishing she had a pair of sunglasses. The metal door slammed shut, making everyone jump out of their skins like a surprise firecracker going off on the Fourth of July.

"Kendra, stick by my side like glue," Jake said with authority, and she nodded her head as the realization of how dangerous their journey would be hit her.

Bill turned toward Julie. "That also goes for you too, my dear."

Julie smiled with a little smirk, making Bill laugh. The four of them began their walk as the sun was rising in the north with the odor of the undead lingering in the air. Bill placed the only key to get back into the school into his pocket, not realizing his pocket had a hole. No one heard it hit the floor, and they walked out of the school.

CHAPTER 12

As the small group walked through the school yard, looking at the motionless swings and the playground covered in dry, crusty dirt, the wind blowing it around the monkey bars, Jake thought that they would never see a child playing there again. It was like walking through the gates of hell. The world would never be the same again.

As the sun rose higher, the strong redolence of decay stung Kendra's nose, causing her to wrinkle it. Jake noticed and handed her a blue handkerchief to cover her nose and mouth with. Tying it in a knot at the back of her head, Kendra, feeling like a movie outlaw, walked with her face covered, holding on to the butcher knife that Sally had given back to her the previous evening to use to protect herself.

Jake was watching for any undead and feeling relief there were none yet, but he knew they were closer than he wanted. The sky was filled with angry, dark-gray clouds, which proudly announced the beginning of a heavy rainfall. The small drops touched his forehead and then his lips, relieving the dryness from the lack of water and putting moisture back into them as Jake licked the wetness.

Kendra pulled the gray oversized sweater Julie had given her over her head to protect herself from the pouring rain. Julie and Bill were surprised as the rain came down in buckets so fast. Only a few minutes before, the sun had been shining brightly in the bright-blue sky.

"Let's go under that huge shrub by the metal gate," Jake said more loudly over the rain to the group as he pointed toward an enormous overgrown shrub next to the gate that led into the school yard.

As the group stood under the shrub, looking around at the new world, Bill watched them huddle close together.

"I am sorry I didn't tell Casey that I loved her when I left. I told her to behave. I should have told her more. That I loved her," Bill said to the small group.

"Bill, she knows that you love her," Kendra said to Bill as she held on to his arm gently.

"I told her not to venture out, to stay in the shelter and not to go anywhere. I pray she listens to me."

Kendra gave Bill a reassuring friendly hug and a smile, letting him know that she understood how he felt and that things would be okay.

Jake overheard Kendra's words to Bill. Believing Kendra had a noble heart, he started to care for her more than he should. He swore to himself not so long ago never to care for another woman since his fiancée was killed by the undead and tried to kill him, breaking his heart in two. When he was near Kendra, Jake felt his heart beat a little faster than normal, which worried him. The rain let up a bit as Jake began to speak. "Everyone, keep close. We are headed to the city now, and there will be corpses there that want to make a meal of us. If anyone spots one, give a little whistle to let the others know. Keep whatever weapon you have close to you and ready to use at any given time."

The stench was at its foulest now that the rain had moistened the blood on the ground. Quietly and watchfully, the four began their journey to the unknown. They all had their own prayers in their hearts as they gripped tightly on to their weapons.

The sidewalks were covered in a bloodbath. Everywhere they walked, there were puddles of blood. Even the windows of the stores, the fire hydrants, and the cars were well coated in blood. It looked like a rainstorm of blood had driven through the city.

"This is a bloody hell," Bill said as he looked at body parts plugging up the grates that let the water out on the corners of the streets—arms, legs, organs, all floating down the streets like paper boats a child would make to float in the water.

Kendra looked down and saw what was left of a torso with only half a head, dragging itself on the blood-covered ground in front of her. The cadaver had only one arm. It reached for Kendra as if it were trying to reach for the skies, stretching it all as far as it could stretch. Kendra gasped as she jumped back a step. Bill walked up to the cadaver and stabbed it in its puss-engorged head. The cadaver was now dead again, but this time, it would stay dead.

They continued to walk toward Clipper Street, which Bill was familiar with. He knew there was a grocery store there once. Kendra readily took Jake's hand into her own. Emotions were flying in her head as she felt safety once again.

The group was a few feet from the corner that turned off Clipper Street, and the stench became horrendous. Jake peeked around the corner as the others stood behind him. Making a sign with his hands and pushing everyone back, Jake whispered, "We have company."

As they turned the corner just a few feet away, there was a family of rotting dead raccoons feasting on a small dog, which was still alive and whining. Jake noticed its tail was still moving. The raccoons began to make an awful screeching noise as they battled for the meatiest chunks of the dog. Each was mauling, shredding strips of muscular meat off the dog's body.

The sounds made the hair on Kendra's arms stand on end. "What the fuck is going on with those damn things?"

"Shut up, or they will hear you and attack us," Jake responded to Kendra in a hoarse voice, which stunned her.

Jake could not believe his own ears as he spoke. He only wanted to protect Kendra. When Kendra didn't respond to him, Jake knew he had hurt her feelings. Not meaning to be so harsh with Kendra, he would apologize later to her. In the meantime, they all had to be extremely quiet.

Turning the corner and silently walking past the raccoons eating the dead dog, Kendra slipped on a mass of vile meat and fell facing a partially devoured arm filled with crawling maggots. Some of them spurted onto her face from the fall. She screamed and tried to stand up. Jake ran to Kendra and lifted her onto her feet as she was trying to wipe the maggots off her face. They stuck on her face like they were glued on.

The raccoons noticed the small group run and snarled as they looked up at them. In one breath, Jake yelled, "Fucking run now!"

As the group ran, the raccoons were right behind them.

Kendra was now running as fast as she could. She tried to keep up with Jake. All the while, she was still trying to wipe the maggots off her face as she held back her nausea and felt bile rise in her mouth.

CHAPTER 13

The shelter was noiseless as Casey sat on the cot with the other girls.

"Let's take a peek outside through the door, Casey. No one will know. We can go as we planned last night," the girl with the red hair said deviously as she looked at Casey.

"I promised my dad I would stay in the shelter," Casey said. Knowing her Dad never broke a promise to her, she decided she would keep her promise to him.

"Okay, fine! Stay here then. I am going crazy here. I need fresh air. I need to leave this hellhole with or without you," replied the red-haired girl who was sitting next to Clara on the cot, looking anxiously at Casey.

Clara was very quiet. She did not want to go with her friend. She had lost her entire family and didn't want to venture out of where she felt safe. She was terrified to go out but was afraid of her redheaded friend at the same time, as she had traumatized her when she slept, telling Clara the dead were right next to her cot and they were going to eat her.

The redheaded girl turned toward Casey with her eyes

slit and an evil look on her face. She said straight to Casey, "I am going outside. No one is going to stop me."

Casey looked at her. "Don't go! It's dangerous out there! You have no weapons to protect yourself. There is no way to get out anyway. My dad took the only key with him."

"Like I said, I want to go out for a few minutes. I am not going out to save the whole fucking world!" shouted the red-haired girl as she stomped away toward the hallway where the heavy metal door was located.

Casey looked at Clara with pleading eyes.

"I don't want to go out there. Casey, please don't let her make me go," Clara said as tears rolled down her face. Clara was the youngest of the girls. She was still wearing the same pink dress as she was when Casey and Bill found her in a garbage can. Bill had accidently knocked it over, causing Clara to scream and jump out when they were running to the school for safety.

"Redhead," as Casey had nicknamed her because she had a fire be bite in her toward people, came back to the gym and once again sat next to the other girls. Opening her hand, she presented a key to the door.

"Where did you find that?" Casey asked.

"I found it on the floor by the exit door, just now."

"Let me hold on to it," Casey said to Redhead as she opened her own hand to take the key.

Clara sat back further against the wall, praying to herself that the girls wouldn't fight over the key. She hated any kind of conflict, as her parents often fought with each other whenever her dad came home drunk.

Redhead furiously placed the key into Casey's palm. She

was planning on repossessing the key from Casey as soon as she fell asleep and then leaving the shelter.

***

Night came quickly, and the darkness filled the gym. The girls lay down in their own cots, trying to sleep, though their stomachs were growling as they were down to one meal a day. Julie had told them the food was running really low and had to be rationed.

Redhead sat up quietly and listened to Casey's soft snoring, indicating she was asleep. Sneaking toward Casey's belongings, she fumbled through her worn-out jean handbag and retrieved the key to the door. Redhead returned to her cot with a strong feeling of control, which she thrived on. She had the key in her hand, knowing it was the only way out of the school.

Redhead packed her measly little bag, which only had one bottle of water and a baggie full of cracker crumbs that she had hidden from the others. She did not want to share her meager food with anyone, no matter who they were. On her tiptoes, Redhead walked toward the hallway to the door while planning on leaving the shelter.

Clara woke up, hearing her flip-flops snapping on the floor.

"Where are you going?" asked Clara.

"I am leaving this fucking place. I can't stand it here another day. I am so over it," Redhead said as she kept walking away from Clara.

"Wait! I will go with you," Clara said to Redhead with a little hope in her heart she would tell her to stay.

"Well, come on now. I'm not waiting all day for you."

Clara took her small bag, which only contained a small hunting knife, and followed Redhead down the hallway. The girls walked down the corridor with the exit sign that hung sideways toward the metal door. Redhead tried the key. It would not open the lock, but after several attempts and Redhead cursing at the door, the key finally turned the bolt. The night was getting dark fast, as the sun was setting, and Redhead knew it wouldn't last. It was becoming dusk fast as the girl walked out of the school.

The door slamming behind them made Clara almost jump out of her skin. The door didn't bolt itself.

"Shush! Be quiet, Clara, or they will hear us."

Clara regretted leaving the shelter. She was tired and wanted to go back to the gym. She started to bawl like a baby.

"Stop that fucking whining! We can't get back in now. The door is shut tight now. Let's get going," Redhead said to Clara in a malicious voice.

The girls did not realize the door never fully shut, not locking after they had left the school.

As the girls walked, the noises of the darkness were eerie and scaring Redhead a little bit as she waited for Clara to catch up to her. Redhead walked fast, babbling for Clara to keep up with her. Clara was younger, only ten years old. Redhead was fifteen and a lot taller and stronger, which was why she terrified her.

The girls walked through the playground. Clara looked downward, toward the grass, which was wet with dew. Redhead walked ahead of Clara, not caring much about leaving her behind as long as she got her own way.

Clara was following behind Redhead, her heart pounding. She had never felt so scared. She was crying silently, wishing she had never left with Redhead. She was picturing the future to be horrible, imagining being eaten by those things. With silent tears, she wished she hadn't left the school. Clara was listening to a tempo beating in her ears. She was also feeling extremely vulnerable outside of the school in the cruel world.

There was a strong predominant odor of death and rotting bodies as the girls walked. Redhead pulled her T-shirt over her mouth and nose. Clara tried to place her dress over her face, but it was futile, as her dress was a summer dress, very thin. It wouldn't help her much.

The girls finally walked to the same beat, close to each other. Clara removed the little pocket knife from her bag. Holding on to it gave Clara a little bit more courage, which she needed. "Redhead, where will we go for the night? We can't get back into the school. Maybe if we banged on the door of someone's house, they would open it and let us in," Clara begged. She was trying to keep up with her pace. Redhead knew she was a couple years older and stronger than Clara, proving her dominance over Clara.

"Keep your scrawny mouth shut. We need to be quiet, very quiet!" Redhead said with vengeance in her voice. "There is no one out here to help us. Just keep going till I say when we can stop."

Clara began to cry fitfully. "I want to go back now," she pleaded with Redhead. Clara was terrified. Her body didn't stop shaking with fear. The night was darker than it had been when they had first left the building. Clara got courage and began to run back toward the school, not seeing a horde of ten undead marauding around toward them. The undead smelled the girls. As they became closer, the moans crescendoed, sounding like a sea of whales feeding on an unfortunate victim. One of the undead, a grotesque, morbidly obese woman, wearing a shredded filthy floral-patterned dress with an apron still clinging to it came at Clara. As Clara screamed, the woman went on a feeding frenzy, grabbing on to Clara and knocking her down hard on the ground. Clara looked up to the woman's hideous face, trying to push her away with her small arms as the pustules of fluid opened on the woman's savage face and flowed onto hers. The corpse screamed in an animalistic voice as more of the undead were behind her, raging mad from hunger and running toward her to join the meager fleshly meal rapaciously.

Clara screamed with all the strength she had, "Help me! Oh my God! Please help me!"

Redhead watched as Clara was attacked and took the opportunity to run free from the frenzy. As Redhead ran, she heard the last of Clara screams as they died down. Redhead was not feeling a bit remorseful for leaving her little friend behind as she kept going.

Clara's last scream ended as the woman bit into her carotid artery and sucked her blood as it pulsed along with Clara's heartbeat. The struggle was short-lived. Clara lay there, unable to fight back as the horde surrounded her and began to rip her body apart and devour her. Clara's last and finale thought was Redhead and how she would somehow get revenge on her for leaving her there to die.

CHAPTER 14

"There, right there, is the supermarket!" Bill yelled out loud as Kendra was running right next to him.

Jake and Julie were not far behind them but a few feet way. Bill noticed the gates were down on the supermarket, which was unusual. They ran to the door next to the store, which led into an apartment building. "Here, let's go in here. We can hold them off with the door!"

Kendra and Julie ran into the small hallway first as Jake and Bill slammed the door shut. They heard the voracious scratches on the door as the raccoons were trying to get in.

"We can try to hold them off a bit, Jake. I will go upstairs and see what's there we might be able to use," Bill said in a shaky voice.

Jake nodded his head, letting Bill know he would be down there, protecting the girls.

Bill climbed up the steep stairs to the second floor, not knowing what mayhem he was going to face. The hallway smelled of old garbage and rotting meat. Bill prayed to himself that there were no undead in any of the apartments as he climbed the stairs faster with a little rejuvenation, wanting to protect himself and the others, like he had sworn to do on active duty before this all occurred.

Several doors to the left of the hallway were closed. Bill looked to the right, noticing one door was open. "Hello? Hello? Is anybody there?" The shaking in his body came out in his voice. Hearing a little shuffling coming from the open door, Bill cautiously tiptoed into a room, which resembled his own living room. It had a large-screen TV on the wall and hanging plants all around. They looked as though they had been there all day, just as if the world had not changed. They were only a little dry and needed some water.

Walking toward what was the kitchen, Bill heard the shuffling noise again, this time a little louder and faster. "Hello? Hello? I am here to help. I won't hurt you." Bill raised his gun, ready for a takedown. From the back of the kitchen, behind the table, a young girl stood up. She looked like she had been there for a while. Her eyes were glazed as she snarled like a wild animal at Bill. Her dress was covered with dry blood and torn. Bill did not want to use his gun on the little girl. He grabbed a steak knife that was lying on the counter, and with tears rolling down his face, he grabbed the girl by her blond ponytail, pulling her head backward, and jabbed the knife into her brain from her forehead. Bill fell backward, crying and looking at the young girl with pity in his eyes. "She was someone's daughter," Bill whispered with tears on his face. Wiping his nose with his sleeve, he was trying to pull himself together.

Jake, Kendra, and Julie witnessed Bill killing the little girl, as they were standing right behind him, not making a sound.

"Bill, get it together! We live in a totally different world. This world belongs to the undead. We have to keep life going on if possible to start a new population," Jake said to Bill in a firm voice, hoping it would connect.

Bill was still in shock, even though he had been taught to handle any situation when it arose. He was not trained for this.

"Okay, it looks all clear now. The raccoons have gone for now. Let's look around and see if there is anything of use. Then we can go downstairs to the supermarket and get supplies to bring back to the school in the morning." Jake spoke to the group, as Kendra was already looking in the cupboards for food.

The small number of canned vegetables that Kendra found was barely enough to feed all of them. But they shared the food, and their bellies were as full as they would get for the time being.

Being late in the evening now, Jake went into the master bedroom, pulled out mattresses, and laid them on the floor. Bill had taken the dead girl out in the hallway.

"We will sleep here tonight. I will keep watch," Jake said. He was the commanding voice of the situation.

Bill and Julie lay on the larger mattress as Kendra lay on the smaller one, which she knew belonged to the little girl, who was no older than five. Covering herself with a blanket, Kendra tried to get some sleep. As she looked at Jake watching out for them, Kendra felt safe.

Kendra woke up startled as Jake lay next to her. She was cold. Even though the weather was warming up, the chill was still in the air. Not knowing what to say or do, Jake covered her up with the blankets they shared. Not saying a word, he just held Kendra and watched while she fell asleep and softly snored.

The sun was rising, and the building was eerily quiet. "Let's go downstairs now. I think those dirty little bastards are gone," Bill said as he rose from the mattress and stretched his arms up, making every muscle in his body wake up.

The raccoons were gone. No one knew were they went to, and no one cared. As they walked outside the building, the stench smacked them in the face once again like a sprinkler in a kids' park. Kendra did all she could to stop herself from bringing back up the meager meal she had eaten the night before. Touching her stomach, Kendra prayed that the baby was going to be all right in this new, atrocious world.

The gate to the supermarket was open. Jake and Bill lowered it halfway down after they entered the store. Kendra was surprised there was no odor of death in the store.

"Look around and stay close," Jake said as Kendra and Julie were heading out already to the canned food aisle. Bill headed to the hunting aisle, and Jake followed the girls and kept a lookout for their safety.

Jake grabbed the empty shopping cart that was just sitting next to the moldy bread aisle. Beginning to fill it up with cans of tuna fish and soup and bringing it closer to the girls, Jake said, "Fill her up, girls! As much as you can. We can wheel it back to the school."

Kendra grabbed a shopping cart from the entrance and went down the baby aisle alone. Her heart was beating as she looked at the baby supplies. Not sure as to what to get for her own baby, Kendra grabbed anything she thought might be needed for Sally, knowing her supplies were low and Alice might have had the baby before they returned to the school.

Bill came around the aisle with a super grin on his

face. They all laughed for a second as Bill was loaded up with every gun you can imagine. Bullets hung off his new hunting coat. "I am ready for hell to rise!" he shouted toward the sky as if shouting toward God himself.

They all heard a screech from outside. Knowing it was a car, they jumped and ran to the front entranceway leaving their shopping carts behind. "That was a fucking car crash!" shouted Jake. "Everyone stay inside the store. I will be right back!"

Kendra held on to Julie's hand firmly.

"Shut the door behind me, and stay inside!" Jake shouted at the women.

The car was smoking, and flames were coming from the front of the car. There was a lot of smoke coming Jake's way as he covered his nose and mouth with his shirt. Walking slowly closer to the red station wagon, Jake noticed someone was sitting in the driver's seat of the car. There was no one in the passenger seat that he could see. Tapping on the window, he whispered, "Are you okay? Do you need help to get out?"

A woman no older than Jake looked up at him and pleaded with her eyes for him to help her get out of the car. Jake motioned Bill to come out of the store to help. Looking around, Bill did not see any undead swarming nearby. The sweat was pouring in rivulets down his face from the fear. Bill shut the large glass door behind him and gave the women a reassuring smile.

They were still holding hands.

Jake pulled on the handle of the car door, and it opened. He helped the woman out of the car. The blood was pouring down her face and dripping on the ground.

"Bill, I think she hit her head petty hard."

The men laid her down on the ground to assess her for injuries. Jake took his shirt off and wrapped it around the woman's head.

"My baby, please get my baby," the woman moaned, trying to look at the backseat. Bill opened the back door, and what he saw was horrific. The baby's face was masticated. All the flesh from its face was gone. Its head moved back and forth as its tongue protruded out of its mouth. Its little legs kicked and fought, trying to get out of the car seat. Bill shut the door; his face turned pale white. Looking like he was going to pass out, Bill turned around and vomited with a painful force all the food he had eaten last night.

"Get her away from the car. The baby is dead." Jake leaned over the woman, noticing her features were changing. "Oh my God! She is dying. Look at her face, Bill. It's changing."

As Jake spoke the words, the woman rose from the concrete and hissed. She reached with her hands toward Jake's face. Bill screamed to Jake from shock, thinking the woman was alive but was going to bite him. Bill ran toward Jake and used his new hunting knife to stab the revolting woman in the head right between her eyes, and she was gone as soon as her head hit the asphalt.

Bill and Jake looked at each other, stunned by what just happened. Then they looked toward the store and did not seeing the women where they were told to stay. They were not there and not to be seen anywhere near the entrance of the store.

"I told them to stay by the window and if anything happened to close the gates and lock themselves in. I don't know where they went," Bill said to Jake as he madly looked around the front of the store for the women. Thinking the worst-case scenario, Bill said to Jake, "Jake, you scout the aisles to the left, and I will go to the right. If anything happened to the girls, whistle to me."

Both men walked toward the back of the store with weapons raised. Bill had given Jake a gun before they went their separate ways, looking for Kendra and Sally.

CHAPTER 15

Redhead ran, as death was chasing her. She ran back toward the school. Reaching the playground, she bent over to expand her lungs, knowing she had outrun the undead but needed the extra oxygen to finish reaching the school. She did not know how she was going to explain what she and Clara done and what had happened to Clara. How would she explain this to Sally?

Reaching into her front pocket, she pulled out the door key. Her only thought was to get into the building safely. She would think of some lie to tell Casey. With a grin on her face, she knew she had made it back to the school. The school had an eerie, dark look to it, as there were no lights on. Redhead could not see where the door they had left from was. She and Clara had left so fast Redhead wasn't sure where the entrance was, so she walked around the building.

Clara rose from the asphalt that she had died on. Sensing she was missing something, she began to walk with her entrails dragging behind her, sloughing on the ground with every step she took. Looking straight ahead, Clara had only one remaining eye, as the other one hung and flopped on her face in rhythm with her steps.

Clara's mouth began to salivate, as she was closing in on the familiar odor she once knew. Redhead began to panic as she banged on the wooden window, which no one heard. Finally, finding the metal door and looking for a bolt she couldn't find, Redhead remembered it only unlocked from the inside. Redhead went into a state of shock. She began running around the school, banging on anything that looked boarded up. She was praying to herself someone would hear her and open the doors. But no one heard her cries other than Clara.

Walking back to the playground, Redhead was giving herself a minute to think things through. Thinking about how she would get back into the school, thinking about running again to a different place but too scared to do that, Redhead's mind was going inexorably. She was petrified being alone in the dark in an empty, eerie playground.

Clara came closer to the familiar odor she knew and began to profusely salivate. She had an impish grin on what was left of her lips when she noticed Redhead with her only observable eye. Redhead sat on the wooden bench where teachers would watch the children play, making sure no child was hurt or any fought with each other. Feeling oblivious to her surroundings, Redhead never heard Clara coming up from behind her. Redhead sniffed the air and noticed a repulsive odor. Looking behind her, she saw what was left of Clara. Clara was alone. She was standing in front of Redhead with drool coming down her chin onto her dress, which was bathed in blood.

Clara's nostrils flared as she stepped closer to her meal. Redhead was flailing her arms as if she were trying to fly. No words were coming out of her mouth. Tears flowed down Redhead's face. It had been many years since she had allowed herself to cry. She now was bawling out loud like a newborn baby. "Clara, I am so sorry! I wanted to help you, but I was scared. I didn't mean to leave you. I swear I didn't," she cried as she stepped back away from Clara.

Praying there was some of Clara still left in her, she begged for forgiveness, as she now stood unmoving. Clara deviously opened her mouth as if to say something, but only her tongue came out. Clara's mouth opened wider and bit hard into Redhead's shoulder. The bite itself burned as if a sizzling coal had landed on Redhead's shoulder. She screamed and tried to push Clara away. The more she tried, the firmer Clara's grip became.

Redhead tried to resist Clara's bite. She realized Clara was too strong. Submission took over, along with shock, as Redhead had no fight left in her and knew her life was over.

Clara gashed Redhead's left shoulder open, leaving sinew and flesh hanging down. Snarling, she dug into Redhead's left breast, ripping it off. Her tender nipple snapped off into Clara's mouth, and she chewed it like she was chewing a taffy from a carnival in the summer.

Redhead closed her eyes as her body felt warm. She felt herself passing on to a new life of death. With opening arms, she identified her passing.

***

Casey awoke, startled, to a banging sound on the boarded window next to the cot where she slept. Looking toward the other cots, she saw neither Redhead nor Clara. "Oh my God!" Casey said aloud, hoping she didn't wake anybody up. Reaching over to her bag, which was hanging off the back of her cot, Casey looked for the key frantically, not finding it in her purse where she had left it. She ran to the exit door.

The door was opened from the inside. Casey could not latch it. Only the key locked the bolt from the inside, and the girls took it with them.

"Oh, what have you guys done?" Casey said aloud to herself as she peeked outside the door. She whispered for Clara and Redhead, but no one answered.

Casey returned to her cot to retrieve her backpack with the few essentials she owned. One of them was a gun with only six bullets left in it. Bill had trained Casey in how to shoot a gun when she was younger, taking her hunting during deer and turkey seasons. It was their favorite sport together. Feeling a wave of sadness and wishing to herself that she had respected him more and listened to him instead of being a bratty teenager, she made a promise to herself when she saw him again she would make it up to him, proving that she didn't have to get her way all the time.

Casey walked toward the school's small cafeteria. She noticed Sally was there creating a concoction for breakfast that smelled unpleasant even though her stomach rumbled for food. "Sally, can I talk to you please."

"Sure, girl. Sit down on the bench here while I cook breakfast." Sally pointed to a bench where Casey could sit. "What is it, girl? Are you okay?" Sally hoped it was just a teenage issue that could be settled fast and easy. Being a cook in the school's cafeteria, Sally was trained to deal with children of all ages.

"Sally, Redhead and Clara were talking about leaving last night before we went to sleep. They were complaining a lot of boredom and being trapped in here. I told them not to go outside, that it was way too dangerous, but when I woke up this morning, they were both gone, along with the only key to the school's exit. I had hidden it in my purse and only the girls knew about it being there. I don't know what to do. Should I wait for them to return, or should I go out and look for them? I know neither one of them had a sufficient weapon on them to protect themselves from the undead."

As Casey spoke, her young face turned pale with fear and worry for the girls out there alone, knowing they were alone and frightened. They should not have gone out to explore.

"Casey, I can't tell you what to do, but for your own safety, stay inside; we don't know what is out there anymore other than death and more death." Sally walked over to Casey and sat on the metal bench close to her, looking into Casey's eyes. "I know what you are thinking and what you are going to do. Please, please be safe out there. I will keep an eye around here and take care of things. If you don't see them, promise me you will come right back. I will be here waiting for you."

Casey gave Sally a huge hug as she cried on her shoulder. "I will be careful. I promise." She placed her backpack on her shoulders and slowly climbed out of a bordered window of the school's safety into the setting sun of the unknown. Sally walked behind her and placed one of the metal lunch benches against the window as Casey exited. "Lord, please be with her. Let the girls all come back safely," Sally prayed out loud.

Casey began to walk toward the small city, hoping to find the girls there. She fully understood where her courage came from—her dad—as she held her head up, looking all around her. She held her dad's gun pointed in front of her. The air smelled of rotting cadavers, Casey noticed, as she placed a well-worn red rag over her nose and mouth. She was thankful she had saved the piece of rag. Her dad had given it to her to wipe her tears away after her mother was attacked by the old woman who lived next door.

***

Casey's mom was worried about the elderly woman next door as walked in through the kitchen to check up her. She had seen the old lady walking around awkwardly as soon as she opened the door. The old woman was sprawled like an animal and attacked her mother so fast that she didn't have time to react. As Casey watched her mom being attacked, she screamed. Her dad came running into the house and shot the old lady in the head. He sat on the floor, caressing Casey's mother in his arms as she bled profusely from the torn flesh on her neck. Casey's mom formed a smile at him, letting him know she loved him.

Within seconds, Casey's mom was dead, and her cloudy eyes reopened with the fierceness of an animal in them. Bill let her go of her quickly. She jumped up like a crazed chimpanzee and pounced on him as he took his handgun out of his safety belt and shot his wife right between her eyes. She fell never to rise again.

Bill walked slowly out of the home as Casey ran up to him, trying to get into the house to see her mother. Bill held tightly onto his daughter, who was crying as loudly as he cried.

***

Casey kept walking closer to the store her father had spoken about as a plan in an emergency, telling her if they ever broke up to look for him there. She was praying that maybe Redhead and Clara are there with her dad.

CHAPTER 16

John had been running from the undead for a week now, praying he would find someone to help him. He was so hungry. He had had nothing to eat for the past three days.

A father of three and a husband, John had lost his whole family when they were boarded up in their home. The news said to stay inside and be really quiet for the time being. But two of the three children decided they were going to fight over the last of the cereal. With all the dead walking around, one of them heard the children fighting. John got his shotgun out from the cabinet, telling his wife, "Get the damn kids in the basement now." His wife panicked and ran down the stairs with the three children, two of whom were not talking to each other.

His wife screamed when she heard the gunshots upstairs and ran to see if her husband was okay. As she entered the kitchen from the basement, the three children huddled close together in a corner of the basement. She ran out of the house to look for John. Not seeing him, she ran back to her children. As she got closer to them, she heard them making funny noises.

"Stop that noise right now. It's not funny!" she scolded them. They did not respond to her words.

John was going mad, shooting at any undead that came near his home. Next door to his house, John saw his friend's wife lying on the ground as her teenage daughter was ripping her intestines out of her stomach and eating them. Hiding behind his car, he shot the girl in the head, and she fell. Just as she fell, her mom stood up.

"What the fuck is going on?" John yelled to himself.

John ran back to his house. Noticing the basement door was open, he was angry. He told his family to stay in the basement, but they did not listen to him. "Carol? Carol?" he called his wife, but she didn't answer. He called his children by their names. None of them responded. John slowly walked down the basement stairs, and to his horror, he saw his three children feasting on his wife. A neighborhood kid was sitting next to them, chewing on her leg.

John ran to his car and drove off, praying to find some help. John drove until his car ran out of gas. From there on, he walked, fighting off the dead as he found them or as they found him. John's overalls were dripping with blood. Most of it was stuck on his arms and legs from the overall ripping. Seeing a school in front of him, John whispered, "Thank God!" out loud. Walking toward the metal door, noticing it was open, John walked into the building.

Sally was making her rounds with the people in the basement when she looked up and saw John. She screamed.

"It's okay, miss. I'm not one of them. I am alive, just covered in blood."

"How did you get in?"

"The door was unlocked, miss. I won't harm no one. I am just hungry and tired."

Sally led John to an empty cot. "Rest here. I will get you some food and a change of clothes."

Everyone in the basement was looking at John in fear, knowing what the real life was like outside. All their dreams and hopes for a new life left them in sadness. John looked around and began to cry uncontrollably. No one came to his side to comfort him.

Night finally came, and the people rested for the night, praying things would change in the morning. John helped Sally place a heavy table in front of the metal door, praying it would hold any undead who tried to come in. "Get some sleep, John. We are going to need it," Sally said as she walked down the corridor to the cots and lay down.

John sat up on the cot. The odor of the undead woke him up.

John shouted, "Get up! They are here! Get the fuck up and run!"

People were trampling over the cots, falling on each other and screaming as the dead ran after them. A few of them made it up the stairs. They were faster than the undead. The older ones became the victims. An older man tried hiding under the heavy blankets but was found when one of the undead jumped on him and he screamed.

It was a massive feast flesh, blood spraying over everything, the undead fighting each other for food. People were screaming and crying; it was a sanctuary of hell. Sally and John ran up the stairs ahead of the others. John grabbed Sally by her arm, shoved her into an open locker, and slammed the door. He ran into the one next to it and slammed that door.

"Be quiet so they don't hear us, Sally," John whispered.

Sally could hear people being attacked in the hallway where they were hiding. Hot tears flowed down her face. She wanted to go help them—that was what she did as a nurse; she helped others—but fear made her hide.

The locker room became eerily quiet after a few hours of the killing. The feeding frenzy was over for the time being. Sally's legs were beginning to cramp after standing for so long.

"John? John? Can you hear me? Is it safe to come out now?"

"Sally, I don't know for sure. We will be taking a chance leaving the lockers. I know they are still out there and know we are here. Hang on. I am going to open my locker slowly. Don't make a sound," John said as he licked the sweat off his lips. Opening the locker slowly, he looked to the left and then to the right, not seeing anything living or dead. "You can come out now, Sally. I don't think they are still here."

Sally and John slowly and quietly walked back down the stairs, as undead looked at them but quickly went back to their feeding. Sally slipped on a bloody step, and John caught her. After leaving the school, they walked across the street. John saw a car that was still running, and they both ran to it. Getting inside the car, Sally turned to John.

"Where are the people who own this car?"

"Hell if I know, but we are leaving now." As the car began to pull away, the sun was setting on the horizon. John and Sally sat in the backseat when darkness came to try to get some rest after several hours of driving.

The night was quiet. No wind blew.

John woke up first. Looking at Sally, he said, "Sally, look up. Look how beautiful the sun is rising."

As John stepped out of the car, so did Sally. They just stood there, holding hands and watching the sun rise. Neither one of them spoke a word to the other.

CHAPTER 17

"Julie, did you hear that?" Kendra cried as the girls backed away from the front entrance, passing the checkouts.

"It sounds like the dead are coming toward the store," Julie responded as she held on to Kendra's arm painfully. "Please, let's go in the direction of the back of the store so they don't see us," Kendra pleaded with Julie.

Kendra knew Jake had told them to stay where they could see them, but she thought it was best to move.

As they quickly walked down aisle 7, the salad dressing aisle, Kendra tripped over a barbecue display. Twisting her ankle, she let out a yell. Julie quickly clamped her mouth and helped Kendra walk to the back of the store, where the rotten meats were.

"We can stay here. They won't smell us with this horrific odor of rotting meat. Sit down, Kendra. I will be right back," Julie said as she ran down a different aisle. She returned with an ACE wrap and wrapped Kendra's now swollen ankle up.

Flies were swarming in the millions around the rotting meat. Kendra and Julie tried swatting them away, but the more they swatted, the more there were. Kendra grabbed a backpack from the outside of the aisle that had an "On Sale" sign on it. She began filling it with cans from the shopping cart, trying not to put pressure on her swollen ankle.

"What are you doing?"

"I am getting as much food as possible, Julie. We might have to run and run fast. I want to at least take some food back with us." As she spoke, she threw Julie a backpack to fill up.

Hearing Bill and Jake yelling for them, Julie didn't answer them, thinking that someone else was in the store and not sure if he or she was dead or alive.

The girls were filling the backpacks up quickly when Kendra noticed a woman walking their way.

"Hello, miss. Are you okay?" asked Kendra as she noticed the woman was dragging her left leg. The foot looked grotesque as it twisted sideways unnaturally. It was puffy and merely hanging on by a shred of skin.

"Miss, are you okay?" Kendra repeated as the woman looked up at her. Kendra saw her face was distorted and drool was foaming from her nose and her mouth down her ID tag, which read Lacey.

"Kendra, run from it as fucking fast as you can!" Julie shouted as she grabbed a can and threw it at the dead woman. Missing, Julie began to run behind Kendra.

"There! Over there is a storage room! Run into it, Kendra! Hurry up! She is right behind us!" Julie yelled.

Kendra ran into the storage room with Julie right behind her. She slammed the door closed in the woman's face.

"Oh my God! I hope Jake and Bill find us in here," Julie whispered slightly out of breath from running.

Kendra bent over, catching her breath. She turned to

Julie. "Where are they? We can't stay in here!" Her face was sweating profusely.

"We are okay here for a bit, Kendra. I'm sure she will leave soon. Then we can get out and find the men."

The dead woman began scratching on the door while moaning loudly, knowing her next meal was only a few feet away from her.

"Just be quiet, Kendra. She will go away," Julie said as she lifted Kendra's foot and looked at it. The swelling was getting worse. "Elevate it on that box next to you, and it will help some." Kendra reached over, grabbing the box of dog treats, and placed her foot on it.

Kendra began to panic. "I don't want to stay here, Julie. I want to go back to find the men."

Julie sat next to her on a defrosted box of French fries, holding her arm around Kendra's shoulder, as the box formed to her body from the fries being soggy.

"We will be all right, and we will get out of here soon, I promise you," Julie said as she rubbed Kendra on her back for comfort.

***

Bill and Jake ran down aisle 7, looking and calling the girls' names. Jake noticed the backpacks full of food on the floor. Hearing a banging noise not far from where he stood, Jake raised the baseball bat that he had found outside on the ground already used, as it dripped blood. His knife was in his left hand, ready to strike at any time, at anything.

"Shush! Bill, I think I hear something," Jake whispered, pointing toward the storage room. He saw the dead woman banging and scratching on the door.

Bill slowly crept up behind the dead woman, holding his breath so as not to breathe in her stench as he stabbed his knife into the back of her head before she even knew he was there. Her blood squirted on Bill's hands and face. "Fucking gross," Bill said as he opened the door to the storage room.

As he did, Kendra and Julie jumped into his arms, almost knocking him down.

"Come on. We need to get out of here before more of those things come," Jake said as he gripped Kendra by her arm to help her walk.

The freezer door opened behind them, and a young man limped out. His name tag said, "Hi! My name is Tom. Can I be of assistance to you?" with a smiley face at the end.

Jake chuckled to himself for a minute. "I will be damned wearing anything that stupid."

The rest of the group looked at him but didn't think it was humorous at all.

Tom was getting closer to the group, and Bill drew out his gun and shot him in the head, spraying blood all over the boxes of cereal on the shelf.

"Why did you shoot him? They will fucking hear it and come? What are you? Stupid?" Jake was getting angry.

"Jake, what the fuck is your problem? Let's just get the fuck out of here!" yelled Bill to Jake as he still held on to Kendra.

"I really wanted that box of fruit rings," Bill said as he made a pouting face when he saw it trickled with gore from Tom's head. The small group walked to the entrance of the store as quietly as possible.

"Stay here," Jake whispered as he opened the front door and looked to the left. Not seeing any of the undead, he waved his hand for the group to follow him.

Jake, Bill, Julie, and Kendra walked close to the buildings to find a place to rest Kendra's ankle. Ready to run if the undead approached, Jake and Bill held on to the backpacks filled with canned food, and Julie helped Kendra walk.

CHAPTER 18

Casey held tightly on to her dad's gun for her life. Not sure where to start looking for her friends, she walked for hours down the hill toward the small city and back up again, looking for Clara and Redhead. Casey was feeling cold and was wishing she had taken a sweater with her. Even though summer was in the air, it was still getting a little chilly.

Casey noticed her favorite clothing store's door was wide open. Stepping inside as quiet as a mouse with her eyes and ears wide open, alert for movement or sound, Casey looked for a warm sweater she could wear. Hearing a strange noise from outside, Casey ducked under a rack of coats that were on clearance. Not knowing what the noise was, she kept quiet for a few minutes, though it felt like hours, as she shook from fear under the rack. Peeping out the window, Casey thought she had seen someone walk by but didn't dare look any further.

***

Kendra and Jake passed the clothing store first, and Bill and Julie walked behind them. Bill did not know his daughter was a meager few feet away from him; he kept moving on.

***

Casey raised her head up to get a closer look. Seeing no one there, she grabbed a dark-brown sweater from a rack, wrapped it around herself, and hurriedly walked out of the store, heading toward the supermarket to look for her dad. It was where they had always planned to meet.

***

As the group walked into the pharmacy that was right next door to the clothing store, they noticed the windows on the door were broken with sharp blades of glass sticking out.

"Be careful not to get cut," Bill said to the group, as he was the first one to enter the store. "Julie, look for anything that we can use in the school. Grab what is necessary for now, and we can come back another time for more," Bill said as he was grabbing bandages and ointments from the shelf in front of him.

Kendra limped to the baby section and grabbed diapers and formula, not for Alice's baby but for her own; her maternal instinct was kicking in. Picking up bibs and little onesies, Kendra placed them in her backpack as Jake watched her with curiosity.

***

Casey stepped quietly out of the clothing store and saw a person standing right in front of her. She stood still with her heart pounding until she looked again and saw that it was her own reflection in the mirror. She began to walk back to the school. Not finding either of her friends or her father, she felt defeated. It was beginning to get darker, and Casey's pace hastened. With every step she took, she heard something behind her, creating a shuffling noise. Casey turned around and faced a little girl no older than five. The girl was bloody from head to toe. She looked to be crying with her head down and shaking. "It's okay. I won't hurt you. What is your name?" Casey asked the little girl as she stepped closer to her.

Casey noticed the bathrobe the girl was wearing had blood dripping from it and prayed that is was not the little girl's blood. The little girl's hair was covering her whole face. Casey wanted to move it aside to see her face but hesitated.

The bathrobe was pink and had an angel embroidered on the front pocket. Casey bent down to the girl's level to try to talk to her again. Within a heartbeat, the girl raised her arms and reached for Casey as if she wanted to be picked up. Casey reached for the girl with her arms stretched out forward.

"Mommy? Where is my mommy?" the little girl cried.

"I don't know where your mommy is, but you can come with me. My name is Casey. I can help you." Casey was happy not being alone anymore and finding this little girl, though her heart broke because the girl had lost her mother like she had.

The girl took Casey by the hand and walked with her down the street. Casey's hand was feeling sticky. As she looked at it, she saw she had blood on her hand from the little girl. Casey raised the girl's hand and noticed it was covered in blood. The other hand held on to a hand that was detached from an arm like a teddy bear. Casey saw it and screamed, scaring the little girl. "Drop the hand!" she yelled as the girl looked at her dumbfounded, not letting go of her mommy's hand.

The little girl walked closer to Casey, and Casey stepped back from her. Within seconds, the little girl's eyes became clouded over and milky white as Casey watched. The little girl's tongue whipped in and out of her mouth like a dog panting on a hot summer's day. Casey was breathless in shock as she stepped back. Not wanting to hurt the little girl, as Casey had never killed anything in her life, she ran away from her. The girl galloped behind her with a hideous face, licking her lips.

The little girl leaped on Casey like a toad leaping rocks. Casey grabbed her hair, pulling her face away from hers and throwing her off. The little girl was slower than Casey thought she would be. As she pushed her down, the girl fell near a garbage pail. Casey grabbed the pail and tossed it on top of the little girl. Using the bag of garbage in the street right off the curb, Casey covered the garbage pail, hoping it would hold the little girl and give her some time until she got away from her.

Reaching into her bag, she pulled out the gun she had carried. Feeling a little safer with it, she held on to it tightly for protection as she hurried back toward the school. It was now completely dark out. Casey had never felt so scared in her life before. The night was evil, and Casey felt it in the air as she cried to herself, praying she would make it back to the school and be safe again.

CHAPTER 19

Kendra filled her backpack with baby objects. Jake continued staring at her. Kendra was not ready to tell anyone that she was pregnant. She was keeping it a secret for as long as she could to protect herself and her baby. She quickly turned her head away.

"We can't go back out there now. It is way too dark. We won't be able to see those things coming. We need to stay here for now," Bill said as he looked out of the broken glass doors. "Those things are lurking out there, and I don't want to meet up with any of them."

Jake and Bill took some of the shelves down after they removed the cans of soup and placed them in front of the store. After returning to the back of the store, the four of them sat soundlessly, silently praying they wouldn't be found. Kendra grabbed a bag of peanuts out of her backpack and handed them out to the group. They had not eaten since the night before. Kendra was hungry, as was the rest of the group. Bill swallowed his down, chased by water and a low burp. Julie chewed on hers silently, making them last as long as she possibly could so she didn't have to think about what was going on around her. She could think of the chewing and the taste of the peanuts. Jake took a handful as he smiled at Kendra. Kendra took a few for herself, put them in her mouth, and began to chew.

She was dozing off on Jake's arm as Julie lay on the floor and Bill looked around the store and listened for any weird, out-of-the-ordinary noises.

Dozing off, Bill heard a crash. "Aww fuck! They're getting in!" Jake jumped up and woke Kendra up as a horde of the undead was breaking into the store.

"The shelves aren't going to hold them!" Julie cried out.

Bill took out his gun and began to shoot the ones that were entering the store as Jake took his bat and began to smash them in the head. Brain matter and blood were all over Jake's face and hands as he hit as many as he could.

Julie grabbed Kendra and headed for the back door. It was locked. Julie screamed, banging on the door, shaking it back and forth, hoping it would open. One of the undead grabbed Julie by her hair, pulling her back into the mass as Jake and Bill were fighting them off. Kendra screamed as she watched Julie being torn apart. Julie's blood sprayed all over the floor. As she screamed, they were dismembering her body, pulling it limb from limb. Julie was still screaming. They were outnumbered. Bill was using a lot of ammo as Jake beat the heads of the undead in.

Kendra ran back to the door, as Jake and Bill were trying to kill as many as they could. She shook the door will all the strength she had. The door opened.

"Bill, Jake, I got the door opened!" Kendra yelled.

Bill ran to the back of the store, seeing what was left of Julie made him run faster. Jake ran to the back of the pharmacy. They all ran through the doorway back up the stairs where they had been previously that day.

Opening the first door, they found a couch and a dresser and moved them in front of the door. The three of them hid behind the smaller couch in what looked like a living room. Jake got up and ran into the kitchen as the others followed. Looking out the window to see if they were being followed, Kendra moved the dusty kitchen curtain over to peek out of the dirty window. Looking at the horde and seeing more of them than she thought were out there before, she panicked. The horde was going in circles, knowing there was food somewhere but not seeing it. They were insatiable, and their moans were getting louder. They were becoming more aggressive to each other.

The three of them sat on the floor in front of the kitchen sink. Jake held on to Kendra tightly as she put her head in his lap. Bill reloaded his gun with sweat pouring down his face. His entire body was shaking from fear.

"This is the last time we are going out! Even if we die in the school, there is no place of safety out here," Bill said aloud in frustration to the others.

***

Casey, walking closer to the school, heard the screams of the undead not far behind her, and the penetrating howl they made pierced her ears. Casey disputed within herself whether to go back to look further for friends and her dad or return to the school, giving up knowing she was her father's daughter. She turned around. Holding her gun in her hand and checking to make sure it was fully loaded and the safety was off, Casey quietly walked back to where she had heard the screaming coming from. She was ready to fight for her life and to find her friends.

In and out of the shadows, she went through alleyways, around cars, within earshot of the undead but not seeing any of them. She kept on walking cautiously. Turning the corner on Clipper Street, she saw a massive horde of the undead surrounding a store. The store looked like a massacre had happened in it from all the blood she saw. The undead were confused by their surroundings, only thinking about their next meal of flesh, like ants to another dead bug.

There was blood everywhere, and torn pieces of flesh littered the ground, sticking to the asphalt like honey sticking to a spoon, making Casey gag. Standing behind an old Ford Escort, Casey leaned on the driver's side, looking over the hood at the horde. Aiming her gun carefully, she fired her gun and shot the closest undead to her. It was a man dressed in a police uniform. The others turned around, hearing the blast but not seeing anyone. They stuck their noses in the air to smell but returned to pounding the door on the apartment building. Realizing taking on a horde that big was next to impossible alone, she backed away from the horde and ran for a few blocks until she was sure they didn't follow her. Seeing an old church, Casey ran up the long flight of steps to the main entrance. On either side of the door, there were small ancient stone bowls that look like birdbaths filled with holy water. She dipped her fingers into one and place the drop of water on her forehead.

***

Kendra jumped out of Jake's arms. "Was that a gun, Jake?"

Jake stood up and looked out the window, not seeing anything but the horde. He wanted to yell for help but didn't want to excite the undead more than he had to.

Bill stood up abruptly. "That is my gun! I know that sound. I taught Casey how to shoot it. We need to go help her and let her know we're here!"

"All right. We need to distract them somehow. Kendra, you go to the back window and start calling them toward the back of the house. Bill and I will let Casey know we are here and safe."

The church Casey walked into to get away from the undead had a musty smell, like old books in a library. Casey slowly walked up the main aisle on the worn-out red carpeting, toward the statute of Virgin Mary. It frightened Casey as she thought it was one of the undead.

The candles on the pew were all burned out and dusty. Casey quietly whispered, "Hello? Is anyone here? I need help!"

No one answered her cry for help. A gray mouse ran across her feet, causing Casey to screech. Angry with herself, Casey decided never to scream like that again over a stupid little mouse. Looking up at the bronze lamps hanging from the high ceiling gave Casey the creeps. Walking toward the front, she considered a door branded "Sacristy Room." As she opened it up, she saw it was a supply room with linen and candles on shelves against the furthest wall.

Casey walked down a small flight of wood steps, seeing a sign that read "Undercroft" with an arrow pointing to the left. She followed it. The room was pitch-black. There were no windows in this room. Casey reached to her right on the inside of the room for a light switch. Finding it, she pushed the button up. The lights flickered on and off for a minute. An open casket lay on the floor in front of Casey. Its occupant was nowhere to be seen. Not waiting to see where the casket's owner had gone Casey decided it was time to leave.

Casey's heart pounded as she grabbed the wall behind her to hold her up and left the basement quicker than it took her to get in. She ran out of the church as fast as she could go. She ran! Just ran! Not knowing where she was going, she was running as if hell itself were chasing her.

CHAPTER 20

Kendra opened the window in the back bedroom. The room was a mess. Whoever had been there had packed clothes in a hurry, leaving drawers open and the bed unmade.

"Hello out there, assholes! Can you hear me! Hello!" Kendra screamed out of the dusty window that looked older than she was. The horde followed her scream as they stumbled into the alley she was yelling from.

"Jake, I don't see her anywhere. Oh my God, what if they got her?"

Bill was frantic with his head hanging out of the second-floor window. He looked for his daughter. "We have to go out there and help her."

"I don't hear her screaming. I think she got away from the horde. We will, Bill. You need to calm down for a minute. We have to come up with a plan first," Jake said calmly.

Bill was pacing the floor, punching his one hand with his other hand, trying to contain himself and think about what to do next to find his daughter. He was positive he had heard a gunshot from his own gun, the one that he had given to Casey.

Most of the horde was now behind the building that Kendra, Jake, and Bill were hiding in.

"Okay, here is the plan. We run downstairs from the apartment and try to outrun them. We head toward the school. Leave the backpacks here so we are lighter and it will be easier to run. Stay together—close together—and have your weapons ready," Jake instructed Bill and Kendra.

Kendra grabbed her bag, knowing there were things that she needed for her baby. No matter how heavy, she was taking her backpack with her. Jake just looked at Kendra as she put the bag over her shoulders but didn't say anything about it.

Together, they walked down the sticky, blood-covered stairs. Jake peeked out of the door, seeing only three of the undead. He enlisted the others to follow him. Bill aimed and shot the three undead in the heads, causing the rest of the horde to run into the alley.

"Why did you fucking shoot?" Jake wanted to say but didn't have the time to say even one word, as the horde was right running toward them—fast.

Kendra screamed, "Run into the supermarket now!"

Jake and Bill were right behind her.

As the trio ran back into the supermarket, Bill handed Jake a gun, saying, "Fuck the knife!" Jake gladly took it and a handful of bullets that Bill handed him. Kendra still had her butcher knife and began to swing it, slicing off half of the head of an undead who was getting too close to her. Jake watched as Kendra fought back, knowing he had a good fighter with him.

Kendra's adrenaline was in overdrive as she swung the knife back and forth, killing as many of the undead as she could. Blood splashed over everything, including herself. Jake took a second to look at Kendra, feeling proud of her. He smiled to himself as he shot the old man who had gripped his arm and was ready to bite. He had no teeth so it was kind of humorous.

Jake, knowing their situation was dire, moved back toward the back of the store behind the meat room. Still, the salivating horde followed them. Kendra did not know where Jake or Bill was as she ran off on her own. She continued swinging her knife. Her arm muscles were burning badly as she fought her way back out of the store into the street. Having no other choice, Kendra ran and ran.

Jake was backing into a corner of a small back room used to store folded-up boxes for recycling. He was surrounded by six undead coming at him all once as he reloaded his gun, surprising himself because his hand was shaking badly. Jake aimed one by one and shot them all. The last undead body he shot had fallen on his shoes headfirst with gore leaking out from his scalp onto Jake's shoes.

"Talk about a close call. That thing is fucking disgusting," Jake said to himself as sweat poured down his back in rivulets like a waterfall.

Bill ran into the back room, shouting, "More of those fuckers are coming!"

***

Kendra stopped in her tracks, looking behind her. She felt guilty for leaving Jake and Bill behind. Holding her knife in the air, she ran back to the store to help them. The store was in a state of pandemonium. Undead bodies were sprawled all over the store. Blood dripped down from the rows and rows of packaged food. An undead, having only his torso left, rolled toward Kendra, snarling and baring his teeth as his entrails followed from behind like a bride's train. This made Kendra feel a wave of nausea.

Kendra heard Bill's gun shooting in the back room. She ran toward the men.

Jake yelled, "Kendra, look out! One is behind you!"

Kendra turned around and came face to face with Charlie again as he snarled, moving his lips and snapping his teeth at her. Charlie was missing an arm from his shoulder joint. It looked like it had been brutality ripped off. Jake raised his gun as Charlie was closing in on Kendra, aiming for his face. He missed and shot him in the shoulder. This only shook Charlie. As his mouth opened wider than humanly possible, getting ready to bite down on Kendra's arm, she held her butcher knife up, ready to cut his head off. Jake came up behind Charlie and shot him in the head from the back. Charlie's head fell to the floor, but his eyes never left Kendra's face.

In agitation, Bill said out loud, "What do you suggest we do, Jake? Put up a stop sign? I'm running out of fucking ammo!"

"Keep moving! Keep fighting these things! Look! There is a freezer there!" Jake yelled as he gripped Kendra's hand and pulled her with him toward the freezer.

Kendra resisted, not wanting to be locked up in the freezer. Jake dragged Kendra forcefully by her arm. "Let's go!"

"No, Jake, I don't want to die in a freezer," Kendra pleaded.

"We are not going to die. We are going to live. We have to go in there for the time being." Jake spoke to Kendra in an encouraging voice. She complied.

"Man, I need a cigarette!" Bill laughed nervously.

"No, man, those things will kill you! They give you cancer." Jake laughed as they ran into the six-by-six freezer, which held frozen food.

"Fuck the cancer, I'd rather fight for my life," Bill replied.

Kendra limped into the freezer, which surprisingly still had a chill to it. As she rubbed her arms up and down, Jake slammed the heavy metal freezer door, catching an undead arm by the wrist. Kendra cut it off with her butcher knife. It fell onto her foot. Looking down, she stared at the separated limb and furiously kicked it across the room. It hit a shelf that was holding melted, gooey ice cream that dripped down onto the floor like a river of chocolate flowing down a mountain, looking grotesque as it poured over the severed limb.

CHAPTER 21

Honk! Honk! Casey thought she was going crazy hearing a car horn beeping. Behind her, a blue station wagon was following her. Casey ran from the oncoming vehicle. The car was beat up on the outside. It was covered in dry body fluid. Casey was frightened as the car caught up to her. She turned around and yelled, "Leave me the hell alone! I don't know you!"

Steven opened the window on the passenger side. "Look, lady! I am not going to hurt you. I thought you might need a little help, being you are the only person out here and you are alone. My name is Steven. I was camping with my parents when all this shit went down. I was only looking for some food, and I won't bother you anymore," Steven said sadly, hoping she would want him around. Being alone was not one of his favorite things in the world, but he began to drive away.

"Wait! Don't leave me here!" Casey said loudly enough to make sure he heard her.

Steven opened the passenger door and invited Casey in with a wave of his hand. Unsure of the decision, she slid into the passenger seat.

"This was my parents' car," Steven said with a huge lump in his throat, missing his little baby brother badly. Steven was happy for the company. He loved the little guy even though he was only six months old. Steven had been more like a father than a brother, taking on a father figure's position when his mom's asshole of a boyfriend dumped her for a younger woman.

"Hi! My name is Casey." That was all Casey wanted to say for the time being, at least until she knew him better. They drove in silence together until they reached a narrow, running river outside the small city. After stepping out of the car, Steven sat on the grass, patting it with his hand. He motioned for Casey to sit next to him. They both sat in silence near the car. There were no undead close by, trying to get to them as their next meal.

"I wish none of this ever happened. It has only been a short time, and the world is in total chaos," Casey said as tears rolled down her youthful face.

"Casey, are you okay? I know all of this is horrible. We will get through it," Steven said as he lay down to look at Casey.

"Where are we going from here?" asked Casey, looking toward Steven.

"I'm not sure. We need to find a safe place to hide. The night is coming, and we don't want to be out there with those dead things."

"How have you been surviving, Steven, for the last couple of weeks? Why haven't you gone to the school for shelter?" Casey asked him.

"I didn't know anything about the school. I thought I was the only one left. I salvaged what food I could find and mostly slept in the car at night, being as quiet as I could."

Steven put his head down and spoke softly to Casey. "My mom and baby brother and I were going on a trip. We were going to show my little brother whales at the Sea Park, even though he was so young. We wanted to take him as a family. As we passed the border, the air seemed a little thicker and had a stench to it. Mom said, 'Don't worry. It smells like a skunk or something is dead.' I turned around to look at my little brother. He was fast asleep in his car seat. My mom closed all the windows and put the AC on."

"Steven, you don't have to talk if you don't want to," Casey said as she moved closer to Steven, seeing his body tremble as he spoke. He needed to talk to someone so badly. Casey knew he was crying when he put his head down.

"I need to talk. I have not spoken to anyone for a long time," Steven said tearfully. "We stopped at a pizza restaurant to get a bite to eat. When we walked in, there were very few people. I thought it was odd because the parking lot was full of cars. I thought it would have been extremely busy inside. Mom and I looked at each, not sure what to do. The people weren't looking good as they sat at the tables; they looked kind of sickly.

"Mom said, 'Let's get out of here. This place looks pretty bad. I don't want to eat here. Besides, it smells like shit here. Let's find another place to eat.'

"As we left the restaurant and walked toward the car, that's when we heard all the screaming, and people were running in all different directions. They were running from something. Mom yelled, 'Get in the car!'

"I grabbed the baby from her. He was crying loudly, scared by all the screaming around him. Before my mom could jump in the driver's seat, a person, a dead person, wild with rage, grabbed her by the back of her head, knocking her to the ground. Before I could run around her side of the car, there were five of those things on her. I could hear her screaming, 'Run, Steven! Take the baby with you.'

"I could not leave her there. I had to try and help my mother. I ran around to her, but the undead saw me and ran toward me. I ran as fast as I could and held tightly on to my baby brother as he screamed. I prayed I would find someone to help us. Those damn things caught up to us. I grabbed a garbage pail lid off the street, and I tried to fight them off." Steven began to cry uncontrollably. "I couldn't stop him. The poor little guy was so scared and confused.

"One of those things came up behind me, knocking me and my little brother. My precious little brother flew out of my arms and rolled away from me. As I tried to crawl toward him, a woman no older than my own mom grabbed him and bit into him, ripping the little guy's legs off. Oh, my God! Casey, she ripped his legs right off!

"I saw my mother, or something I though was my mother, walking toward me, growling like a dog. I pushed her and jumped into the driver's seat and have been there since. I have not left this car but only for a few minutes."

Casey placed his head on her lap while rubbing the back of his head. She let him cry his emotions out. Casey felt weird holding on to a total stranger, but this was the way the world was. Life was precious! Living people were precious.

Casey began speaking as Steven sat up, feeling relieved that he had the chance to talk about the horrific events that he had gone through. "I was home with my mom and dad. My mom wasn't feeling too good. We thought it might be the flu. My mom was an emergency room nurse at the local hospital in town, the only one there is for miles. When she came home after her twelve-hour shift, she began to really not feeling well. The emergency room was packed that day. It looked like the whole town had the flu all at once. She had admitted fifteen patients to the medical surgical floor that day."

Casey continued, "We were planning on going out for dinner at the town's Chinese restaurant. My dad was hoping that if Mom ate something, she might feel better. My dad was off that night. He worked an eight-hour night shift as a cop. Sometimes he would come home with horror stories. Sometimes his nights were quiet. For the past week, he kept talking about a new illegal drug that was driving people crazy. The jail was full, and there was no place to send the prisoners, so they were cramped together in one cell.

"We pulled into the restaurant, hoping my mom would eat something that would make her feel better, even if it was just broth. When we walked into the restaurant, the odor slapped her in the face. We turned around and headed out. My mom fell on the ground walking down the steps. She began to convulse with foam coming out of her mouth. My dad kept yelling her name, but she didn't respond. I tried calling nine-one-one on my cell phone, but all the lines were busy. Mom's arms began to flail all over, as if she were about to take off and fly. My dad pushed me away from her. Then she just went limp. We thought it was over and she would be okay, but when she opened her eyes, they were all white. She snarled at me like a crazed animal." Casey was now crying too. "My mom jumped on all fours and looked at me with drool rolling down her chin.

"My dad said, 'Don't look, Casey! For the sake of God, don't look at her!' As I placed my hands over my eyes, I heard a bang. My dad had shot my mother in the head and killed her. I ran to her as my dad grabbed me by the arm. 'That is not your mother anymore, Casey. Let's get out of here and find a safe place for the night.'

"It was all a nightmare to me. We drove around until we saw a group of people running toward the town school. My dad stopped the car, and we ran along with them. As soon as the last person was in the school, the door was shut and locked. People were crying and screaming until one man yelled for everyone to shut up. The hallway became eerily quiet with little sobs left in the air. My dad grabbed me as we walked together down the hallway into the basement that had a huge yellow sign that said 'Shelter.' Everything and everyone I ever loved is dead, gone! Life will never be the same again. I don't know if I can live like this," Casey said tearfully as Steven put his arms around her and together they walked toward the car.

"I left the school to go out and look for my dad. He left the school a few days ago, for supplies, and has not returned yet. He usually comes right back within a day or two."

"I think we need to find a place to stay tonight for shelter. I don't want to hide in the car anymore," Steven said as they sat back into the car, shutting the doors.

"Steven, look over there," she said, pointing to the church doors, which were still open. "I wonder if it is safe in there for the night," Casey with enthusiasm.

Steven noticed the inner church doors were also open as he went up the long flight of stone steps. "Stay in the car until I come back out and let you know that it is safe in there," he said as he turned back around and headed up the rest of the stairs.

As Steven walked into the church, he pulled out his Zippo lighter and held it high in the air, looking around for the undead. Not seeing any, he walked back to the main entrance, waving his arms, letting Casey know it was safe in the church.

Walking close together toward the back of the huge church, they saw a closed door. Steven opened the door quietly with Casey holding tight onto his arm. She knew she had been in this room before but didn't want to let Steven know how scared she was and that she had run out. Casey noted a cot near the furthest wall and walked toward it. He grabbed a sheet he found hanging off a wooden chair right behind the door. Steven and Casey, exhausted from the day's events, lay next to each, breathing in unison as they both fell fast asleep.

CHAPTER 22

"Those fucking things are trying to get in here!" Bill yelled as he held his body's weight against the metal door."

"Bill, they can't get in here. The door is too heavy," Jake told Bill as he was bending over Kendra, looking at her ankle.

"It's okay, Jake. I can walk on it. We'll be okay," Kendra said in a low voice, not even believing herself that her ankle would be okay.

Outside the freezer, it sounded quiet. Jake didn't hear anything, and neither did Kendra or Bill.

"Do you think they're gone?" Kendra asked Jake as he replaced a semifrozen bag of string beans on her ankle after taking off the melted bag of corn.

"The swelling sure has gone down, but just keep it elevated," Jake said as he walked toward the door.

Bill sat up, feeling stiff from lying on the cold floor. Shaking his body back and forth to get his blood flowing again, he walked toward the door and stood next to Jake.

"Man, what do you think, Jake? Do you think those

fucking things are gone by now? We have been in here for hours. I can't take the cold in here no more, man."

Jake turned toward Bill and gave a little snicker. "That is because you are an old man, Bill."

Kendra giggled as she rubbed her sore ankle. She stood up and walked up next to Jake. Putting her right ear against the door, she said, "I don't hear anything on the other side of the door, Jake, and I think we should leave this store. The sooner the better."

"Jake, I can't stand another minute in here. I am freezing to death," Bill said.

"I'm going to open the door slowly. If you or Kendra see any undead, slam the door quickly," Jake said in a low firm tone. He walked out of the freezer first, looking to the left and then to the right. Not seeing any undead, he motioned for Bill and Kendra to follow by waving his hands toward them. Kendra was nervous as they walked out further and further into the store.

Walking down the cereal aisle, Bill grabbed a box of Fruit Loops while looking at Kendra and Jake. "These were always my favorite when I was a kid."

Jake looked back at the freezer, making sure the carbon box he had placed between the door and the freezer was still there in case they had to run back.

The setting sun was shining brightly through the store's large windows in the main front entrance. One window by the door had a smear of blood making it look like a small rainbow after a rain shower. Kendra stared at it for a minute, thinking how beautiful a rainbow really was and wondering if she would ever see one again in her life. Next to it was an undead who could barely walk. His mouth was open as he grossly licked the window while he looked at the small group. The flesh on his face was mangled, hanging off his chin as if his whole face had been scraped off with a sharp knife. His nose was broken and making an eerie sound as the bone scraped against the window. His tongue then went in and out of what was left of a mouth like a crazed animal trying to taste the flesh it could not reach. His arms were raised in the air, as if he were trying to push the window open, seeing the undead so weak, he didn't worry Jake so much.

"God damn! Fucking gross!" Jake said as he looked at the undead, making him feel sick to his stomach. "Let's sneak around the thing while it's busy licking the glass." He looked at the open door. He grabbed Kendra by the arm and pulled her outside with him. Not seeing any more of the undead for the time being, Jake and Kendra began to make a run for it. "Let's head back to the school!" Jake yelled as they ran.

Kendra squinted her eyes against the bright sun's glare as she shielded them with her hands.

"Jake, do you think they left and went somewhere else for food?" Kendra asked as he pulled her to run faster.

"Kendra, I don't know! Let's just run away from here," Jake replied.

Bill's face turned pale as he looked at the horde of undead coming straight toward them.

Kendra yelled, "Bill what's wrong?" as she followed his eyes toward the mass of the undead.

Bill yelled, "Don't look! Keep running! Run for your lives!" Bill ran ahead of Kendra and Jake. Kendra was falling a few feet behind; her ankle was beginning to really hurt.

As they ran through the alley filled with garbage, Bill ran to the left, leaving Kendra and Jake way behind. Jake looked behind them, seeing three of the undead closer than he thought they were.

Grabbing Kendra by the arm, he yelled, "Look! There!" He pointed to a garbage bin.

Running as fast as he could, Jake soon reached it and opened the lid.

The smell of rotting garbage hit them in the face. "Jump in, Kendra, now!" Jake said as he held her by her arm and pushed her into the bin. He jumped into it, slamming the lid down and holding on to it.

"We will stay here until it is safe to get out," Jake said as he placed his shirt over his nose and mouth with one hand. Kendra, gagging from the stench, held her mouth and nose with her shirt. Tears fell down her face. The dead knew the two were in there, and they moaned and groaned from hunger. Food was close, but they couldn't get to it. The louder the moans were, the faster the tears fell down Kendra's face. Jake reached over and held on to her as he held the lid down, trying to comfort Kendra as best as he could while the banging on the bin continued.

Jake was beginning to feel responsible for Kendra. He had to make sure she made it through all this horror safe, though he did not know why he felt this way.

The moaning began to quiet down, but the undead were still outside of the bin. Jake heard the shuffling of their feet. Kendra had dozed off, Jake, not wanting to wake her up yet, also fell asleep himself. Kendra woke up feeling her arm going numb. Seeing Jake asleep, Kendra gently shook his arm, waking him up.

"Jake, wake up. I think they're gone now," Kendra whispered.

As she shuffled her body in the foul garbage, she made herself gag.

"I think we need to make it back to the school so we can clean up. We both smell like shit," Jake said as he slowly opened the lid to the bin.

"Where is Bill?" Kendra asked as she looked up and down the small alley between two brick buildings.

"I don't know, Kendra. The last I saw of him, there were about ten of those things after him. I hope he is okay and made it to a safe place."

Jake helped Kendra get out of the garbage bin while he looked around for any undead. Jake walked to the exit of the alley. Not seeing any undead, he motioned for Kendra to follow him.

"You smell like shit!" Kendra said to Jake.

Jake looked at her with a smile, as if to say, "You do too," but he didn't want to upset her, knowing how sensitive women could be. Kendra had lost her knife in the bin and was feeling very vulnerable without it. Jake was still holding his baseball bat and stepped forward into the street. He held it up in the air, ready for action.

***

Bill looked behind, and not seeing Kendra or Jake, he ran into an old shoe store.

CHAPTER 23

"Jake! Jake!" Someone was yelling his name.

"Kendra, did you hear my name called?"

"Jake!"

Kendra heard it this time.

"Look, Jake! Over there by the church. Someone is waving their arms at us. It's Casey with someone else," Kendra said as they walked toward the church.

Jake grabbed Kendra's arm and ran to the church. After running up the long flight of steps, Jake gave Casey a huge hug.

Casey was hugging Jake back, crying. "Where is my dad? Jake, where is he?"

"I don't know, Casey! We got separated, but I'm sure he's okay."

"Let's get out of the open and back into the church where it's safer."

After they all walked into the church, Steven locked the huge wooden doors behind them. Casey sat down next to Jake in a second-row pew, hoping he knew something about her dad. Jake looked at Steven.

"This is Steven. He found me walking around, looking for my dad. He has been with me since."

Steven nodded toward Kendra and Jake.

Kendra stared at Steven for a few minutes, knowing she knew him from somewhere but not sure where. Letting it go for the time being, Kendra kept his face in the back of her mind. Who he was would come to her.

"There is a basement here. It has some food in it but not much. Blessed crackers and a few bottles of water are better than nothing."

As Jake stood up, looking around momentarily, he felt like the statues were staring down at him, as if they were alive and watching every move that he made. It gave Jake the worst eerie feeling and made his hair stand on end. Shaking the eerie feeling off, Jake turned to Casey. "Let's get out of here and go down to the basement. I don't like it up here."

Casey and Kendra stood up together walking out of the pews as the men walked ahead of them toward the back of the church.

"What is the plan, Jake?" Steven asked as they walked down the small, dark hallway.

"I have no idea, Steven. My goal is to stay alive if I can. We will figure things out as we go. That is what I have been doing since all this shit started," Jake said.

Casey and Kendra sat on an old well-used, worn-out red satin couch with stains all over that smelled like mildew. Kneeling in front of Casey, Jake looked her in her eyes.

"Casey, I don't know what happened to your dad. I promise you we will find him. I am sure he is alive somewhere safe. You know your dad is a smart old man," Jake told her.

Casey cried as Kendra pulled her close to her shoulders.

She let Casey cry it out. Kendra knew what it was like losing someone you loved dearly.

Casey flipped her long blond hair up into a sloppy bun and was feeling a bit relieved that Jake and Kendra were there with her and Steven.

"Kendra, don't take this personally, but you stink awful. We should see if there are some clothes in the donation box. I believe all churches have them," Casey said as she moved away from Kendra.

"I know, Casey. We were hiding in a garbage bin for a while, a long while. I can't stand the odor myself," Kendra responded while wrinkling her nose.

Casey and Kendra walked back down the small, dark hallway. Casey had seen a door earlier but didn't dare open it alone. Kendra eyed the closet door up and down, wondering if she should just open it or call for Jake. "I'm going to open it. Stand behind me, Casey," Kendra said as she turned the gold-plated doorknob.

Kendra slowly opened the door. It wasn't a closet but another small room. Looking around, she decided it was too dark to see. She went back to the room where Steven and Jake were talking. Grabbing a candle, she headed to the room where Casey was waiting. Steven and Jake looked at each other with a questioning look. Kendra opened the creaking door all the way and stepped inside with the candle ahead of her. Kendra's heart was beating almost out of her chest. Casey held on to Kendra's arm tightly, walking closely behind her. The horrific odor smacked both girls in the face at the same time.

"Kendra, what is that smell?"

"I don't know. We will find out though. Stay close to me," Kendra replied.

Kendra found another door, and they walked toward it. The odor became worse. Kendra turned the knob slowly on the closet door with her heart almost coming out of her chest. On the floor of the closet there was a closed black bag labeled "Donation." Kendra grabbed it and passed it to Casey. Clothes were also hanging. They looked like priest's robes, so Kendra just left them be. Behind the donation bags, there was a puddle of gross ooze, Kendra noticed. Knowing that was where the odor was coming from, she said, "Let's get out of here, Casey. I have a bad feeling about this closet."

Kendra stood and exited the closet. Looking at the clothes that hung up, she noticed where the bloody ooze was coming from. There hanging from the pole was a dead priest who had hung himself. His neck was twisted in an inhumane way. Kendra opened her mouth and puked up what little food she had in her stomach. It was mostly bile, which burned her throat, and she spit it out. She screamed, "Casey, grab the bag!" She slammed the closet door shut, reminding herself never to open this door ever again.

Both girls ran out of the room. Kendra grabbed a box of matches that were on the rusted, white metal table next to the closet. Shutting the door to the room, Kendra and Casey looked at each other with relief that they were out of the room safe. Kendra ripped the bag open and prayed she would find something that would fit her. Carefully pulling out the clothes, Kendra found a pair of sweatpants and a sweatshirt that was a little too big for her. She was relieved that the clothes would cover her growing stomach. Kendra was not ready to let anyone know she was with child. The infant was growing in her womb every day. After grabbing a pair of jeans and a T-shirt for Jake, hoping they would fit him, they walked to the room where the men were.

"Thank you for the clothes, Kendra," Jake said as he lifted his filthy shirt off and replaced it with the clean one. "Girls, close your eyes for a minute," he said as he was undoing his pants.

"What was the screaming about?" Steven asked.

"In the closet, a priest had hung himself. I guess prayers didn't work for him either. He is still in there. I shut both doors tight."

After a brief meal of dry cereal and holy crackers, downed with small sips of water, the small group sat quietly by the lit candles in the tiny room. In their own thoughts, Kendra and Casey fell asleep on the well-polished wooden floor. Jake covered them up with priest's robes that were lying across the back of the couch.

Kendra was the first to wake up, having to go to the bathroom more frequently as the baby was pressing on her bladder. Jake, unable to sleep, watched as Kendra left the room.

Quietly walking behind her, not wanting to scare her, he whispered, "Kendra."

Kendra turned around toward Jake, a little startled.

"I was just going to find the ladies' room."

"Do you mind if I go with you, Kendra? I don't want you walking around alone!"

Kendra nodded.

The two walked together, looking for a restroom.

"Look over there." Kendra pointed her fingers to two closed bathrooms; one had a figure of a male and the other one of a female.

"Let me go in and check it out before you go in alone,"

Jake said as he began to open the door to the ladies' room. After a few minutes, Jake walked out. "All clear, Kendra. I will wait here for you."

Kendra was feeling a little uncomfortable with Jake right outside the door; nevertheless, she had to pee.

Coming out of the bathroom, Kendra thanked Jake. "Jake, do you know why all this is happening to the world?" she asked as she overly wiped her hands with the paper tissue from the bathroom, as if she could wash all the germs from the world off.

Jake and Kendra walked back to Steven and Casey, who were still asleep. They sat on the couch. Jake allowed Kendra to put her head on his shoulder while he rubbed her upper back.

"Not really! Let's try to get some sleep," Jake replied. "I will never understand the human race and why it does what it shouldn't and messes with Mother Nature."

***

Jake woke abruptly, startling everyone in the room. "Be quiet! Do you hear that?" There was a shuffling noise in the hallway right outside the room. "It is one of those fucking undead things," he said in a low voice as the Kendra and Casey moved behind him and Steven. Jake grabbed a butcher knife from the floor where Kendra was sleeping. He opened the door slowly, and the stench hit him in the face.

Casey and Kendra were holding on to each other tightly as they stood close to the back of the room.

"Hello? Hello!" Jake said in a low voice as he put the light of the candle in front of him and walked out of the room. Steven grabbed a golden candleholder that was sitting on the coffee stand in a ready position for attack.

"Oh, my God! It's the dead priest from the closet. How the fuck did he get out?" Kendra yelled as she stared at him in shock.

The priest shuffled toward Jake. The side of his face was mangled from pulling his head out of the rope that he hung himself with. His teeth were grinding together as if he were already chewing flesh. His head was hanging by a small piece of neck skin. As he walked, his head bobbled back and forth. His eyes were focused on Jake as he came closer.

Steven ran from behind Jake and hit it in the head with the golden candleholder. This only made it more pissed off. As Bill hit it, the skin on its forehead peeled off like he was carving a turkey on Thanksgiving. The piece of flesh hung over his eyes, and he just kept shuffling. Steven walked up to the priest once again and stabbed him in the eye with the back of the candleholder. He pulled it back out, and the priest's eye came along with it. Steven shook the candleholder until the eye fell off.

Kendra turned around and violently vomited. Casey walked up behind her, holding her hair out of Kendra's face.

"Are you okay, Kendra?" Casey asked.

"Yes, thank you, Casey," she said as she noticed Jake watching her.

"Jake, I think it's time for us to leave this church. We don't have any more food here, and it stinks like hell."

"I think you're right, Steven. What do you girls think?"

"Let's grab what we can, get out of here, and go back to the school, maybe," Kendra replied. "I don't want to stay here anymore. This place gives me the creeps."

"Okay, guys, pack up what we can and head out of this place." Jake was glad to get away from all the statues, which he felt were watching him.

All four began to walk out of the church toward the school.

Casey said, "I need to find my dad."

"Change of plans for now," Jake said as he grabbed Kendra's hand and ran like hell from another horde of undead.

CHAPTER 24

Bill kept running from the horde of the undead, not seeing Kendra or Jake behind him. He tripped over a partially devoured arm and spotted a broken piece of wooden board next to it. "Thank you, Jesus," Bill said aloud to himself. He grabbed it, jumping back on his feet like a scared spider and swinging at the two undead who were catching up to him, hitting the closest one in the head and knocking it down. As he hit the other undead in the face, the blood splattered off like a water sprinkler.

Other undead were after him with mouths salivating for his flesh. Bill ran into an old shoe store and slammed the doors shut tight behind him. Snapping their teeth and stretching their boney, fleshy fingers, they tried to grab him.

"You're not going to get me today, you bastards," Bill said aloud toward the group of the undead. Sweat pouring down his face, Bill grabbed a wooden table on which shoes were repaired. As he pushed it against the door, the dusty shoes slid off. A shoe stretcher caught Bill's eyes. He grabbed it and held on to it so tight that his hand turned white.

Bill walked toward the back of the store. "This is insane,

the end of the world and the only thing I have to protect myself is a fucking shoe stretcher."

He moved the green, musty curtain over to look outside the filthy window. Seeing the dead all around behind the store, he knocked over a dead flower with his elbow. Looking at the plant, Bill noticed a pair of rotting feet behind a small table. Walking closer, he saw there was a body of a dead woman with her intestines hanging out of her stomach, dried up and grotesque. Burping up and swallowing his own bile, Bill felt tears fill his eyes.

Looking further, Bill saw a dead man with a hole in his forehead and the look of frozen terror on his face. Between the bodies, there lay a baby no older than six months, frozen in death.

Bill jumped as he heard a thumping on the window. Peeking out, he saw an undead woman wearing a bloodstained sundress trying to break the window, knowing that he was in there. Taking a chance, Bill ran back to the front of the store, not seeing any of the undead who ran toward a huge apartment building directly across the street from the shoe store.

Jumping up to reach the fire escape, Bill climbed up until he reached the landing. He sat down, waiting for his heart to stop palpitating so fast.

He shivered in his shirt from the sweat and climbed through the window. He saw blood splattered all over the kitchen walls, cabinets, floors, and stove. As Bill placed his foot on the floor, he saw a trail of blood with pieces of flesh leading out of the kitchen. The stench was horrific. He covered his mouth and nose with his sweaty T-shirt, only making the smell worse.

Walking over the bloody trail, Bill sat on a fluffy green couch. As he sat down, he saw dust bunnies bounce out of the couch through the sunshine in the room. Leaning back for a second, he listened with ears wide open for any undead. Looking toward the open bedroom door, he sat up and walked into the bedroom. After looking around the bedroom, Bill moved the sun-bleached curtains over to see what was outside.

Not seeing any undead for the time being, Bill opened the drawers to the larger of the two dressers. They contained a woman's clothing. After closing the drawer, Bill began to open the drawers of the smaller dresser. The top drawer contained men's clothing. He began to undress and removed a pair of socks. He walked to the closet and removed a man's outfit of a shirt and pants. Luckily, they fit. He was extremely happy to remove his own gross clothes.

Bill walked back into the kitchen and opened the refrigerator to see a bottle of whiskey. "Damn!" Bill yelled as he helped himself to a large gulp. Back in the living room, Bill pushed the couch toward the door, lay down, and sipped on the whiskey. He fell asleep on the couch by the door after looking at the blank television and wishing it work. Nothing mattered as long as Jack Daniel's was by his side.

Awaking up with a headache, Bill was angry at himself for falling asleep. Sitting upright, he noticed the darkness had taken over. Not hearing any undead, Bill went back out the same window he came in and down the ladder. He ran back through the alley, still holding on to the shoe stretcher. This was his only means of protection against the undead. Bill thought he heard a truck's engine as he ran into the alley. It was too late. Two men jumped out of the trunk and ran toward Bill, One man shot the undead that was chasing Bill.

Bang! Bang! Bill ducked as he heard gunshots behind him, praying as a bullet hit him in the leg and knocked him down. Before Bill passed out cold, he heard strange male voices speaking incoherently. He felt a sharp pain in his head before he went semiunconscious.

"Put him in the fucking truck!" a male voice yelled.

"No, you put him in the truck. This was your idea," a different male voice replied.

That was all Bill heard until he woke up again hours later while the men were dragging his body. He had no idea what was happening to him.

CHAPTER 25

Bill's eyes had begun to flutter as one of the men had a flashlight shining in his face.

"Is he alive, Harold?" a voice asked.

Bill heard a man's voice. As he tried to talk, Bill realized his mouth had something nasty-tasting stuck in it. His arms and legs wouldn't move. They were tied up. Bill began shaking his body from side to side, trying to get the ropes loose. Needing to ask what was going on, he gagged as he tried to spit the rag out of his mouth.

"Relax, dude. You are not going anywhere anytime soon," said the taller of the men, whom Bill guessed was the leader.

Bill looked around the small, dim room, not seeing much of anything but a small wooden table in the corner with a knife sticking in the top. He looked behind him. There was a dead woman, a young girl wearing a summer dress. Bill didn't see any of her body turned from being dead.

"She was shot in the head," Harold said as he saw Bill staring at her. "It keeps the meat from turning."

Bill wasn't sure if he was hearing right. *Keeps the meat from turning?*

Sweat poured profusely down Bill's face as he realized the two men were cannibals and he was on their dinner menu now too.

The younger brother bent over the woman lying on the floor and removed her wedding bands. Biting into them with his rotten teeth, he smiled.

"Yep, this here is real gold."

Bill felt bile building up in the rotten gag. Shaking his head to hold the bile worked for a bit.

"What the fuck are you doing? Leave the dead lady's wedding band. It isn't worth shit!" Harold yelled at his younger brother, Jedd.

"Aww, man, can I at least have her for a bit before we panfry her?"

"No, get your ass over here and help me lift her onto this damn table, and leave the damn rings on her," Harold said in a pit-fire voice.

As Bill watched the brothers communicate, he knew he was in deep shit and being tied down like an animal wasn't helping either.

Harold pulled the gag out of Bill's mouth, fiercely ripping it out, causing a piece of Bill's bottom lip to go along with it. Harold tore the small piece of flesh off the rag and put it in his mouth, sucking on it with a grin on his face.

"You're a sick son of a bitch! What are you going to do with me? Let me go!" Bill yelled. His throat was dry and his mouth hurt from them shoving a gag in it.

"Shut the hell up before I put this gag back in your

mouth. No one can hear you anyway. We are underground in a storm shelter."

"Fuck you, man! Help me! Someone help me!" Bill screamed at the top of his lungs as Jedd came behind him and hit him in the back of head with his fist, knocking him out cold.

"Jedd, let's get this shit done. Put the bitch on the table. I'm fucking hungry."

Bill felt the whack on the back of his head. "God! Please protect my daughter! My daughter!" were the last words that came out of Bill's mouth as his head hit the concrete floor.

***

Jake and Kendra walked out of the church slowly and quietly. Casey and Steven followed closely behind. The sun was bright as it hit Kendra's eyes.

"Jake, are we going back to the school?" Kendra asked.

Jake was looking straight ahead at an ambulance. He noticed something moving behind it. Not sure of what, he pointed to the group to stay back so he could look. Behind the ambulance was an undead, just barely able to walk, shuffling its feet as it held on to the side of the ambulance. Jake came up from behind it and stabbed it in the head with the butcher knife, killing it for the second time.

Steven jumped into the driver's seat and started the engine. The motor sputtered a few times before it started. He yelled to the others, "Get in now! Let's get the fuck out of here! More of those things are coming our way!"

Kendra jumped into the back of the ambulance, and Casey jumped in the front passenger seat, slamming the door behind her.

"Drive to the school, Steven!" Jake yelled from the back of the ambulance, as Steven began driving.

Reaching the school, Jake knew something was not right. The hair on his arm was standing up.

Looking at Kendra, Jake said, "Stay close to me."

Steven parked the ambulance in front of the school. Jake and Kendra stepped out. As the small group walked closer to the school, a horrific odor hit them.

"We are going in with extreme caution," Jake warned them.

Casey held on to Steven's arm tightly as they walked toward the school.

Jake opened the steel door that should have been locked. The metallic odor of blood smacked them in the face. Kendra's heart was beating fast from fear.

Steven slipped on a severed arm and yelled, "What the fuck was that?"

"A fucking arm, dude, get off the floor. Let's keep going," Jake replied with a tremor in his voice.

Jake and Steven walked through the metal door into the school first. Jake noticed the cots were thrown around, and blood was splattered everywhere he looked, like a bloody holocaust.

"Do you think anyone is alive in there, Jake?" Steven asked.

Passing the basement and walking around the cots carefully, Jake held on to Kendra. Walking up the cement stairs, holding on to the metal handrail, Jake was ahead of the group with his bat ready to kill what was already dead. Behind Casey, an undead began climbing the stairs in a spider walk position with her legs and arms going in the same rhythm with each other. Her tongue protruded out, moving back and forth in an irregular way. Casey saw how fast she was climbing the stairs at her and screamed.

Her eyes were glazed and fixed on Casey as she licked her salivating, rotten lips, getting ready for a divine meal of flesh. Steven shot the undead woman in the forehead with Casey's gun, and down the steps she went for the last time.

Reaching the second floor, Jake looked ahead to see if there were any undead there. As he walked down the corridor, a horrific odor was thick in the air. Kendra held on to her nose, trying not to smell it, holding her sick stomach at the same time. Blood stained the ceramic floor, making it look shiny from the sun seeping through the windows at the end of the hall.

Casey whispered, "I hear a noise coming from downstairs."

The group turned around toward the noise. It sounded like an animal in pain. Steven walked down the stairs first. Casey was right behind him.

Sitting on the floor behind one of the cots in a far corner no one looked at earlier was Alice, the pregnant girl. All the group could see were her legs. They were shaking and moving around abnormally. Steven walked toward Alice as silently as possible. Then he saw the blood and heaps of it. Alice's stomach was brutality ripped wide open, leaving a cave where her infant grew. She was still alive, coughing up blood. She looked up at Steven with pleading eyes.

Steven looked up and saw the older couple sitting together in a small closet added to the basement, eating the infant. They had ripped it out from Alice's stomach. The older man was sucking on the infant's thigh like a popsicle on a hot summer day, and the older woman was devouring pieces of flesh she tore off the infant's abdomen.

Behind Steven were Kendra, Casey, and Jake. Kendra looked at the infant and began to cry uncontrollably. Casey grabbed her by the arms.

"Take it easy, Kendra. Don't lose it now; we have come too far."

"The baby! The baby!" Kendra kept saying as Jake took her away from the grotesque scene and sat her down on an upright cot. He quickly browsed the rest of the shelter, seeing if there were any undead, wondering where the rest of the people were.

Steven let Alice come closer to him while he raised his knife, prepared to kill her. Alice was reaching out to him with her bloody stomach as it dripped copious amounts of blood and her intestines on the floor. Steven thought for a moment she was alive until he looked at her cloudy eyes. Walking up to her, Steven stabbed Alice in the forehead, making sure his knife entered her brain.

Jake inserted a knife into the older woman's headfirst and then quickly did the same to the old man. Neither put up any kind of fight.

Kendra sneezed. As she did, the small group of undead from the second floor heard her. They began to run to the basement shelter.

Jake shouted, "Get the hell out of here now! Run!"

Casey was the first one out the metal door. She fell on the ground, tripping over a bloody limb, twisting her ankle painfully. Steven grabbed her by the arm and dragged her with him until she got her bearings so she could run on her own with a limp. Jake and Kendra were close behind. The group ran south together.

"No, keep running. They are too close to us to stop."

"Steven, I can't run anymore. I think my ankle is broken," Casey cried to Steven as he held her hand, trying to help her run.

"Casey, we need to run! You have to! They are right behind us!" shouted Steven.

***

Kendra and Jake were way ahead of them. Kendra looked back, looking for Casey and Steven.

"Jake, where are they? They were right behind us!"

Jake looked back, not seeing either Casey or Steven. "We have to keep going, Kendra. If we go back, we will die! I just pray they are okay."

"No, we have to go back!" Kendra said as she began running back toward where they came from. Kendra heard a loud woman's scream.

Jake grabbed her by the arm. "Kendra, it is too late for them. Come on. We have to keep going. I'm so sorry."

Tears were freely flowing down Jake's cheeks.

***

"Steven, I can't go any further," Casey said as she sat on the grass and looked at her swollen ankle. She screamed as she looked back, seeing how close the undead were. Steven picked her up and ran with Casey in his arms.

Seeing an open door to an old bakery, he ran through it, shutting the door behind him. He dragged a cake display rack over and placed it against the door. Once again, he picked up Casey and went into the back room, praying silently there were no undead in the store. Beside an old bakery oven, Steven sat next to Casey as she cried.

"We will be okay, Casey. I promise you," Steven said as he put his arms around her, trying to calm her shaking.

CHAPTER 26

"Where are we going?" Kendra asked Jake, as they were exhausted from running from the undead.

"Oh my God! Jake, look! Someone is reflecting the light with a mirror," Kendra said as she pointed to the bright lights.

Jake noticed an old, beat-up minibike balancing against a maple tree. After removing the dried leaves off it, he said, "Kendra, look here. We can ride this to where the light is reflecting. It could be people, people who are still alive and want to help us."

Kendra and Jake sat on the rusted bike. Jake turned the key. As it started, Jake kicked off the brakes. As it sprang into motion, Kendra held on tight to Jake. They took off.

Riding past houses with boarded-up windows, Kendra wondered if there was anyone else alive inside of them. Some of the houses were still smoldering from an ongoing fire. Kendra coughed from the smoke. She held tightly on to Jake, fearing what the impending future would be.

"Let's stop here for a minute and take a break. We are safe for the time being, and it's still pretty early and light out," Jake said.

They sat next to an apple tree. Jake grabbed a few apples and handed some to Kendra. She ate one, not taking a break as Jake watched her. Kendra could remember the last thing she ate.

"Little hungry, are you?" Jake asked Kendra.

She looked up at him, and the tears flew down her reddened face. "Jake, I should have told you before all this." Tears continued to roll down Kendra's face. "I was going to but didn't want anyone to worry about me."

"Kendra, please tell me what is it," Jake said with fear in his face.

"I am three months pregnant. I was going to tell my husband, Aric, while we were on vacation, and then all this happened. He never knew he was going to be a dad."

Jake sat next to her. "Kendra, the baby can still have a dad. I won't leave you! We can raise it together if you want. There is something special about you. I noticed it the first time I saw you. We are going to make it. Okay? Trust me. We will find a safe place and raise the little one together."

Kendra reached over and hugged Jake. "Thank you."

"Let's keep going, Kendra. It might take a while before we reach the flashing light. Take some apples and put them in the back of the pack in the small storage box, and I will fill my pockets up with some," Jake said as they mounted the bike.

Kendra and Jake rode for what seemed hours. The light was still flicking and was closer to where they could see someone holding it up.

Reaching the light, Jake noticed a scabby, dirty man was holding a mirror, which was reflecting the sun. Rising from his beach chair, which had seen better days, the man spoke to Kendra and Jake. "Howdy, folks! Glad you saw the reflection! My name is Harold. How are you all doing today?"

Jake was uncertain what to say. He was in shock at seeing another surviving person. Harold lifted a wooden door that was concealed with dry grass. If anyone went by, they would never have known there was a shelter buried underneath.

"Thank you so much! We are so happy to see other people alive. My name is Jake, and this here is Kendra. We drove quite a ways following your light. I can't thank you enough. It's pretty rough out here, as you know."

"Well, folks, it's getting a bit chilly out here. Let's head into the underground shelter that my brother and I built years ago. Boy are we ever glad we did. My mom always warned us that the world was going to end, and boy we are sure glad we listened to her," Harold said in an overly cheerful voice.

Climbing down the ladder, Jake went first and then Kendra. Harold was the last. Jake watched as Harold locked the lid to the underground shelter.

"Only for protection, folks, so none of those things get in here," Harold commented as he noticed Jake was staring at him.

"Jedd! Jedd! Get these here folks something to drink." Harold spoke louder than needed.

The shelter was bigger than Kendra had imagined it to be.

Harold showed them around. There was a full bathroom, two bedrooms, a living room, and two spare rooms that Harold didn't show them.

Harold ushered them into the living room while Jedd came in with two bottles of water. Kendra looked at Jedd and felt bad for him, knowing he was mistreated by his older brother as he bowed when he was told to get water.

"You folks stay here and relax. I will get you a bite to eat."

Jake and Kendra looked around the living room. It looked cozy with a soft, cushioned love seat, which they both sat on; a small television set, which was turned off; and a few pictures hanging on the walls that must have been their family members.

"Now go on and get finished up with the work you started a while ago, Jedd, and do it right this time."

Jedd nodded his head, and he walked into a small room quickly and shut the door tight.

Kendra looked at Jake, hoping he smelled the same thing she did. The odor was coming from the closed-door rooms. Kendra motioned for him to look at the door.

"It is probably the utility room and the wires smelling," Jake said to console Kendra. "Stop being nervous and try to relax. We have traveled a long way to get here."

"You folks relax. I will throw something together for dinner if you all are planning on staying for a bit."

"Thank you," Jake replied, not sure if they wanted to stay there or move on. The place was creepy.

Kendra stood up and walked closer to the door.

"Jake, it reeks badly. Something is dead in there, I believe. Come here and smell."

As Jake stood up to go to Kendra, he heard a loud thump in the other room where the door was also shut. Jake ran to the room and slowly opened the door. Kendra stood behind the closed door on the other side and screamed as she looked at mutilated human body parts hanging up as if they were smoking it like beef or pork.

Turning around and running into Jake, she noticed Bill tied up. Jedd was cutting up a woman on the table in the far corner. Butcher knives were hanging up on the wall with blood dripping off them. The woman was still alive, as her body trembled on the bloody table. Bill looked at Jake with renewed strength. Jake grabbed the hatchet that hung on the wall behind where the door opened.

"Kendra, untie Bill now."

Jake punched Jedd in the head with all the strength he had and knocked him out. Slamming Jedd on the floor and grabbing the butcher knife, he stabbed Jedd in his chest where his heart was. Jedd grabbed the woman off the table to cover himself against Jake as Jake reached to stab him again in his chest. Missing, he cut Jedd's arm off from the shoulder.

Jake grabbed Kendra by the arm. Bill stood up and stretched his sore muscles. They ran for the exit. Bill had begun crying profusely when he saw Kendra and Jake.

"Hey there! Not so fast. Don't you folks want to stay for dinner?" Harold said with a demonic grin as he raised a shotgun toward the small group. Jake grabbed Kendra and put her behind him.

"Like fucking hell, we do!" Bill replied to Harold as he was getting closer.

"Kendra, get behind me!" Jake yelled as Harold ran into the living room.

"I got this bastard. He is mine. Get up the ladder and open it. Get out of here!" Bill yelled to Kendra and Jake.

Harold jumped on Bill, punching him in the stomach. Bill's police instincts kicked in, and he rolled Harold off himself, punching Harold repeatedly in his face with all the strength he had left from being tied up to a kitchen table for days. Bill knew life was not safe with assholes like him around.

"Bill, come on! I got the lid opened!" shouted Jake as he helped Kendra get out of the shelter.

Pulling herself up, she reached for Jake. Kendra was yelling, "Bill, come on! There are some of those things out here. We have to run!"

Bill didn't respond for a few seconds. Jake grabbed Kendra's arm and ran as Bill climbed out of the shelter. He was being pulled back down by Harold. Bill screamed as the undead jumped into the underground shelter, forcing both Bill and Harold back in.

Kendra bent over. "No! No! No!" she yelled.

"Come on, Kendra! We must go!"

The two of them ran into a small town where there were dead everywhere they looked.

"Look! Kendra, we need to get out alive. Can you run into that building?" Jake was pointing to an old apartment building. "I will fight them off and meet you in that alley over there by the large dumpsters, I need to know you are safe."

"I don't want to leave you!" Kendra cried.

"You have to so I can fight them. Just go and meet me there in an hour or so. I will whistle for you. Go now! Run!" Jake instructed her as he led the horde of the undead away from her.

Kendra ran up the steps two by two. Seeing an apartment door open, she ran through it, slamming the door behind her. Running to the window, she looked for Jake and didn't see him. Wanting to yell for him, she didn't. Opening one of the kitchen drawers, Kendra found a long Cutco knife. Holding on to it for dear life, Kendra sat down in front of the stove and waited for Jake's whistle.

Kendra awoke after a few hours of sleep, which she could not fight any longer. "Oh my God! Did I miss his whistle?" Kendra cried to herself.

Looking out the window, she couldn't see anything. It was too dark. She only heard the moaning and groaning of the undead. Falling back asleep, Kendra woke up with the sun shining in her eyes. The world was quiet outside now. Kendra stood up and stretched her muscles as she walked to the window, still holding on to the long knife. Not seeing Jake, she walked out of the apartment and quietly down the stairs, trying not to touch the blood on the handrails.

Walking through the broken front door carefully, Kendra whispered, "Jake! Jake, are you out here?"

She stretched her neck, looking for him.

Kendra's heart was beating so fast she thought it was going to pop right out of her chest. Her hands were shaking and sweaty as she held them together. Finding it hard to breathe, Kendra forced herself to take deep, small breaths. Looking down the alley where Jake said to meet, Kendra saw him. Her heart jumped with joy. He was walking weirdly, slumping to one side. His right shoulder was hanging like he had gotten an injury during the fight. Kendra watched for a few minutes, feeling bad that he looked so tired.

"Jake, are you okay?" Kendra called in a shaky voice.

Jake didn't answer. Kendra figured he was tired from fighting the undead all night. She walked up behind him, slowly reaching for his hand with her shaky hands.

"Jake, are you okay?" Kendra said with fear in her voice.

CHAPTER 27

In slow motion, Jake first turned his body and then his face toward Kendra. As Kendra looked at Jake's face, she made a loud gasping noise. There was no skin left on his face. What flesh he had left was hanging in shredded pieces still attached to his facial muscles. Jake's eyes protruded from their sockets in a revolting way, with hunger, looking straight at Kendra.

Kendra froze as she went into a semicatatonic state from shock. Letting out a bloodcurdling scream, she fell hard to her knees. Jake lifted her face with his bloody hand and bit into it, ripping flesh from her cheekbone. Kendra did not put up a fight. Looking up to Jake, she watched as he chewed on her flesh. She did not scream, knowing this was the end of her life. Her time had come to an end in this world for. There was no more fight in her.

As the sun rose, Kendra saw Jake slowly swallowing her face. She knew this world was a place of living hell, and there was no more fighting.

Kendra lay on the ground, slowly closing her eyes. The intense pain began. At first, it was unbearable. The nerves in her body attacked her as they began to die, one nerve at a time. Tears were pouring down the sides of her face.

She had no body control and didn't feel her tears flowing down into her hair, which was covered in blood. Kendra could not wipe them because her hands didn't move. Trying to focus her eyes on the rising sun, she could not tolerate the burning of the sun's brightness.

Kendra tried to scream, but her vocal cords were numb and dying. She felt her life begin to drift away, and the pain ceased. Kendra began to convulse violently with her head hitting the cement as her blood flowed into puddles along the alley of what was once a beautiful city. She gurgled on her own blood but could not taste or swallow it.

She stumbled to stand up. Rigor mortis had taken over her body. Every extremity was stiff and difficult to move. Looking at her fingers, she was unable to feel them as the numbness had taken over. Feeling the pain of insatiable hunger in her stomach, Kendra looked at Jake, and he began to walk away from her.

"Ugh" was the only verbal sound that came from her bloody mouth. She stood behind Jake. The new world was now theirs. Together, they walked into the midst of the living. Kendra smelled flesh in the air, in the warm, gentle breeze. She now saw the world behind her dead eyes as she followed Jake, seeking the flesh of the living.

Kendra's dream was to own a home for herself and her husband Aric as they were starting a new family. After a short visit to her Mom's house, the world turned into hell for Kendra. Losing all that Kendra loved that meant anything, she learned she had to fight for her life and the life of her unborn baby. With an inner strength, Kendra never imagined she had, killing the undead has become a way of life now for Kendra. As she and a few close friends travel through hell as the living dead chase them wanting to devour their flesh. Follow Kendra through her journey of the living hell.

Acknowledgments

I was born in the big city of Brooklyn. As a child, I loved to watch horror movies and read horror stories. My dream of writing a horror story came true, and I am so happy to share it with other horror fans. I pray you enjoy it much as I loved writing it.

I would love to thank my grandson Anthony Mariani for drawing the book cover for me; my daughter, Courtney, for her advice and encouragement to write my dream; and my husband for all his patience and understanding when I was a little frustrated and for listening to my horrid thoughts through the book.